SACRAMENTO PUBLIC LIBRARY
828 "I" Street
Sacramento, CA 95814
02/18

Bodies of Summer

WITHDRAWN
FROM THE COLLECTION OF
SACRAMENTO PUBLIC LIBRARY

D0976581

MARTÍN FELIPE CASTAGNET

BODIES OF SUMMER

Translated from the Spanish by Frances Riddle

DALKEY ARCHIVE PRESS

Originally published in Spanish as *Los cuerpos del verano* by Factotum Ediciones in 2012.

Copyright © Martin Felípe Castagnet
Translation copyright © 2017 Frances Riddle
First Dalkey Archive edition, 2017
All rights reserved

Library of Congress Cataloging-in-Publication Data
Identifiers: ISBN 978-1-62897-1-620
LC record available at https://catalog.loc.gov/

Partially funded by a grant by the Illinois Arts Council, a state agency

www.dalkeyarchive.com
Victoria, TX / McLean, IL / Dublin

Dalkey Archive Press publications are, in part, made possible through the support of the University of Houston-Victoria and its programs in creative writing, publishing, and translation.

Printed on permanent/durable acid-free paper

"There is no heaven or afterlife for broken down computers; that is a fairy story for people afraid of the dark."
—Stephen Hawking

1.1

IT'S GOOD TO HAVE A BODY AGAIN, even if it's the body of a fat woman that no one else wanted. It's nice to be able to stroll down the sidewalk and feel the texture of the world. I like to cough until I'm hoarse and inhale the smell of the used clothes in my bedroom. The heat saturates my skin. I squint my eyes. Until recently any light at all was too much for me.

My son Teo's grandchildren help me take my first steps. They carry my battery; they twirl around laughing. Our route goes from the house to the corner and back. They clap for me when I make it all the way. I rub the head of the littlest one and say "What bright hair you have." My voice sounds strange to me.

Teo makes gestures from where he sits on the front steps. He opens his mouth but his old age impedes him from speaking. He smiles and nods his head. I take my son's hand; it's swollen and feels like a bag of ice, but it has a firm grip.

1.2

I decide to go down to the kitchen in the middle of the night. The side effects of returning from flotation are insomnia and extreme hunger. My grandson's wife left me a bowl of cereal and fruit for after dinner but I finished it immediately.

Wales insisted that I sleep in the master bedroom on the ground floor but I said I'd be more comfortable in the guest room and the doctor allowed it. Now I regret the decision as I drag my battery on wheels down the staircase; it makes a lot of noise. The lights are off. I sweat. I bang into things; I could easily fall and ruin this body if I'm not careful.

Even after living so many years in flotation, this house still feels like my home. But everything has changed. It's as if I've returned after a flood, like a wave has washed over the surface of everything, moving the appliances, staining the walls with new colors, and deforming the furniture.

I have to stop to catch my breath as I make my way to the kitchen. The refrigerator is full of things I can't eat until I finish adapting. A screen indicates the strength of the wi-fi connection. The fridge is aware of its contents: any item added or removed will register on its inventory. I quickly close the door so that I'm not tempted and because the light makes me blink.

The oranges are kept in the same place but in a new basket. The silverware is now put away in a different drawer. The knife I used so many years ago is still just as sharp; it must be a different one. I don't recognize the plates. I pull out a new chair and sit at the old table. A strange difference:

the house was falling apart before but now it looks shiny and new. Someone named Cuzco comes in to clean on weekdays. I haven't met him yet.

I peel an orange; the smell reminds me of my father. I slowly pick the white skin from each slice before I put it in my mouth. I separate the slice into smaller pieces with my tongue. I suck on the seeds like pieces of candy. I spit them out like chewing gum.

I trip over my cord and get tangled up in it as I make my way back to my room. I'd prefer not to have to carry this battery around but it's the only model my family could afford. I pause in front of the bathroom mirror: I see an old woman, short and fat, supernaturally pretty.

1.3

As soon as I was alone the first thing I did was put my fingers in my vagina. I didn't feel anything. I lay in the hospital bed staring out the bare window. I saw my battery for the first time, plugged into my body like a leash between a dog and its owner. The doctors wanted me to sleep. My mind felt fresh even though the head had been used before. If the brain had any memories, they had been erased. My knees didn't work yet, but the rest of my new body did. The mind interprets the release from flotation like the cessation of a cramp. The absence of my penis, however, feels similar to the phantom limb syndrome that amputees sometimes suffer.

1.4

Teo's grandchildren ask me to play soccer with them. I explain that I can't, that this body is fragile. "Imagine that my skin is like a banana peel." The soccer ball is a star that pulls me into its orbit. I should move out of the way but I remain rooted to the ground at the edge of the garden. The ball comes toward me. I stop it with my foot but I don't dare try to kick it. It burns my hands as I throw it back to the boys.

I instinctively begin to smile as I wet myself. At first I'm confused; I try to interpret the change in my body as if I were diagnosing a strange noise in a car engine. Then I relax and enjoy the sensation under the warm midday sun. I don't want to move, not even to go to the bathroom. I don't want to leave the sun. I am a tree, its trunk pissed on by a dog.

A few minutes later the wet diaper begins to irritate my skin which is swollen from the heat. I'm ashamed to ask my grandson's wife for help. September has a research grant and she works at home most of the day. She takes me to the bathroom to change my diaper. She's used to helping my son Teo, her father-in-law. September doesn't remember, doesn't want to remember, that I was her age when I died.

1.5

The glow of a computer fills almost every room. My psychologist says I'm allowed to connect in small doses;

internet withdrawal after leaving the state of flotation can be painful. I feel tempted by the web even in front of the refrigerator. I resist the impulse purely out of fear. I wouldn't know how to work the touch screen, the keyless keyboard, with these fat hands.

I prowl each space of the house illuminated by a screen. When I can't stand the urge to let the web suck me in like a mosquito sucks blood, I retreat to the only room that doesn't have a connection. Teo is sitting on his bed. His sentences are short; he has to break words into syllables as he catches his breath.

"Na-ked in the pour-ing rain."

I try to fill in the pieces as best I can: "Are you remembering something from when you were little?"

He nods his head. "On my na-ked horse." He moves his hands slowly. I think he must be hot and I hand him a glass of water. At times he's more lucid than others. He's often reliving a past that I wasn't able to share with him. It was Adela who took them on camping trips after I'd already gone into flotation. I would anxiously await their return so that the kids could tell me what they'd done. I've saved the register of every conversation; I could read them now if I dared to connect.

I leave Teo's room as he murmurs something about a baby and a screen door. I walk to the computer as fast as my battery will let me. I sit within the range permitted for the verbal indications that guide me through the web with my ridiculously scratchy voice. I want to avoid touching the cold, transparent screen. I could swear that it smells like blood, like amniotic fluid. I know that my senses are overstimulated after returning to the house where I lived an entire life. My dead wait for me online.

1.6

It's strange to be on the outside. I look at the screen as if it were an aquarium. I used to be a fish and now I walk again on land. I find my friends, some cousins, coworkers. Many of them died shortly after I did but others have only been dead a matter of weeks. Some of them will eventually decide to return to a body; others won't ever want to come back.

The internet is now totally personalized, but never private. Each search leaves an indelible digital mark that's as easy to trace as a footprint in the snow; visible to the living as well as the dead. When I first entered flotation the dead were encapsulated in modules that you had to pay to access. Now, they all float freely along the web.

I come across friends I've never met in real life; in life. I worry about how they're going to treat me. They might reject me now that I have a body again. There's a certain comradery among the dead, like there might be among the deaf, among scientists of the same discipline, among fans of the same movie; we're veterans of a war that extends into a permanent truce. "Hello, Rama!" They greet me as if nothing has changed at all. A few days outside of flotation, overwhelmed by so many soft surfaces and bitter smells and sour tastes, and I've already forgotten what it's like on the inside.

But today I don't want to talk to them and Vera is unavailable. I don't feel like reviewing all of our old conversation histories. What I really want, with a desire so strong that it punctures my eardrums and bursts my appendix, is to track down my former best friend, and to find out what happened to my wife.

2.1

THE STATE OF FLOTATION is the maintenance of brain activity inside an information system. It's the first step necessary to save an individual consciousness. After death you can then proceed to the second, optional stage of migration from one support to another: from the web back into a physical body. This process is referred to as "burning" a body. The first stage is as secure as the second is unpredictable. The physical body, molded to the needs of its first user, must learn to move in the ways dictated by its next guest. This adjustment involves a delicate balance; cellular memory can be deceived, but only up to a certain point.

2.2

The majority of the dead decide to enter a new body. Others choose to remain on the internet indefinitely. A smaller minority return to the original body that rejected them, like a beggar bound to his rags; they are considered demented. Only a few of the elderly refuse to participate in the process. My son Teo is among them. He isn't even a statistic.

2.3

Legal and Biological Restrictions for Reincarnation:

All reincarnations must be recorded in the Koseki Register.

Minors cannot be burned into adult bodies.

A person must first die in order to obtain a new body.

A body may be sold to the highest bidder.

2.4

When I went through the process of entering into flotation, my body was destroyed. At that time they hadn't yet figured out how to conserve bodies and burn people into new ones. The technological advances we've seen since then have been astonishing. First, mothers began to put their children on the waiting list for new bodies, just in case they were to die in an accident. Bodies came to be seen as a valuable natural resource. Funerals became a thing of the past. Then, obituaries started to include information about who would be reincarnated in the body of the deceased. Finally, it was decided that cemeteries should be destroyed. Most were converted into community gardens, due to the fertility of the soil. The few cemeteries that remain now function as museums.

Each body has an average life span of three inhabitants until it finally deteriorates. Then it's cremated. Some families prefer to eat the remains of their loved ones' bodies instead of selling them to be used by other people. This is only legal if it's been authorized by the deceased in their will.

I guess this is the future.

3.1

MY OLD BEST FRIEND is not only old because he was young when I was too, almost a century ago, but because he's not my best friend anymore, he's not my friend at all. I haven't even talked to him since then but I know he has to be alive somewhere. This certainty shakes me from my lethargy. Every day now that I'm awake, and even when I was in flotation, I ask myself the same question: what is the ultimate revenge now that death no longer exists? I bite the fingernails of my new body. I rip off the tips and spit them on the floor and they start growing back without my say-so.

3.2

Days pass without any significant events. Meanwhile, the new body has its demands and I do morning exercises to strengthen my muscles. September writes while I lift weights. I can hear the grinding of my joints through her silence. The window to the study is open; she's inside and I'm outside. The house is large but we like to be close to each other.

"Will you stay with me, Rama? If I'm alone I get sleepy," she said the first time. The boys are at school all day.

She doesn't seem to be afraid of living with a dead person. I ask her if she believes in ghosts.

"Of course," she responds without looking up, "ghosts who lift weights in my overgrown garden."

"I meant the ones who don't have bodies."

"The ones in flotation."

"The internet counts as a body. The internet is thick, translucent, unstable." As I say it I imagine a jellyfish. Millions of seaweeds protected forever inside the bell of a jellyfish. "It's the ectoplasm."

September offers to make me some tea but then she remembers that I can't have it yet. I ask her if she could bring me a glass of water so that she'll stop apologizing. I rest the weights on the patio tiles and the bench sticks to my shorts as I sit down to wait. A thread of sweat runs between by breasts; I run my finger down it and then I bring it to my mouth. It's salty. I hear September returning and I pray that she didn't see me.

"The sun is making you red," she says.

The glass is covered in condensation, as if it were sweating too. I empty it quickly and I hand it back to September. I pick up the weights off the ground. September doesn't return to her desk immediately; she remains standing, just inside the window, her hand shading her eyes. Her hair shines like in a shampoo commercial. Maybe she wants to have some girl talk, I think anxiously. I don't know if I should put the weights back down, I'm afraid that I'll break the spell and she'll leave. But I don't know if I should continue exercising with her standing there.

"Wales never liked to talk much about his family," she

tells me, "maybe because it was such a big one. For him this house full of relatives and memories was always a burden."

"And the spirits that come back from the dead?"

September sits on the floor, hiking up her skirt a little to avoid staining it with the red dirt and the yellow fruits from the trees. "You built this house," she answers.

"My father was an architect; he started teaching me his craft from the time I was your kids' age. We began designing this house when I was a teenager, so that it could be for me and my family. He died before we even got started and I had to build it on my own. I guess Dad liked the idea of living with me and his future grandchildren after he retired."

September lowers her hand whenever the sun goes behind a cloud. Her eyes are so similar to an ex-girlfriend I once had that I'm afraid to check if they're related.

"And what about your mom?"

"A car ran over her when I was nine years old."

"I'm sorry."

"Sometimes I think how different my life would have been if flotation had existed back then. My mom could have stayed with me, on the internet or in another body, somewhere. Dad used to tell me that Mom was in Heaven; back then religion was all we had. But you can't access Heaven by computer. Religion isn't user-friendly."

"The Church has been more accepting of flotation recently. Even though they think it's an evil process, it does prove the existence of the soul."

"At least they're not excommunicating the people who enter into flotation anymore."

"They performed exorcisms on the first reincarnated."

We laugh. September lowers her hand to cover her open mouth. She has the first noticeable wrinkles of adulthood around her eyes and on her hands; the sun lights them up. I have more wrinkles than her, but my body is at least ten years older.

"Why didn't you sign up for a body as soon as the procedure was legalized?" she asks me. "Why did you stay in flotation for so long?"

"A person can get used to anything, even a prison cell, and especially if the prison is pretty comfortable."

I'm still holding the weights and even though they're resting on my thighs, my hands start to hurt. I bend down to set them on the ground; the effort leaves me panting. I have trouble getting my hair out of my face. I never was good with hair and it's even trickier in the body of a woman.

"Hold on," September says as she kneels down to help me fix my hair. Her hands are warm and I try to focus on the patio tiles which look like mandalas while she has her face so close to mine.

3.3

There are things that make me regret not having registered for a new body as soon as possible. But I don't know how to explain it to September.

I'd been on the internet for sixty years when Vera died. I loved Vera the way parents love children that take their time to arrive. My firstborn, brilliant, generous Vera. I speak of her in the past but she's in the state of flotation, almost always asleep, but always lovely. One day, if you can count the succession of events inside the web in days, Vera showed up among us with the candor of a tourist visiting a foreign country. No one from the outside had warned me. "What happened?" I asked her several times. She didn't know how to read me, maybe she hadn't yet figured out how.

Could September understand that I didn't have the physical strength or willpower to make the arrangements for a new body? It's the everyday effort, imperceptible for the living, of maintaining all the muscles together and all the nerves coordinated, both eyes pointing in the same direction, the tongue away from the teeth, the bladder active over the toilet, inhaling the right amount of air and exhaling as much as necessary. Nothing is truly automatic; pain can trigger a process but pain can be suppressed as well.

Once I read that African slaves used to commit collective suicide because they thought they would be reborn in Africa. So the owners mutilated the bodies to scare the others. This is how we lived: the fear for the future body halts our illusions.

3.4

September returns to her desk. She's read part of her research project to me. When she can't seem to explain certain parts that she considers obvious I remind her that it's been almost a hundred years since I was in school.

The level of knowledge you pick up in the state of flotation is incalculable but it's not highly specialized. Nowadays many of the dead are taking courses in online universities. I should have done it but laziness is invincible, not even death can overcome it.

Teo's bell rings: just once, it's not urgent. I offer to go myself. September thanks me several times. I enter the house happy to have an excuse to abandon my exercises under the hot sun. The battery makes new noises as it rolls over different surfaces. The hallway is cool and it smells like lemon cleaner. I try to follow the traces left behind by the mop but the moisture evaporates from the heat. My son's room is at the end of the hallway, the closed door that the internet doesn't pass through.

Teo is standing, clutching a piece of furniture as if it were a railing. In my hurry to help him I trip over my battery. I'm so heavy that it's hard to pick myself up. The old man looks at me with curiosity. When I manage to raise myself up, he holds onto my back to help himself back to bed. "Rid-ing a hip-po-pot-a-mus," he says. Muffled against my neck I hear his unique laugh that seems like it comes out of his nose or ears. I put him in bed. He gestures for me to cover him with the bedspread; when it reaches his neck he seems satisfied.

"What did you call for?" I ask as I sit on the chair next to the bed; for a second I'm afraid it might collapse. He shakes his head and covers his face with the sheet.

"I've been searching the internet," I say; the idea of consulting him comes to me as I start doing it, "but I haven't come up with anything significant." I can only just see his hair and his eyes, black as oil. "I've been searching for your mother for over sixty years actually. For all that time I could only do it by internet. Now I can finally search for real, all the leads have dried up. Vera never wanted to tell me anything. You told me you didn't know, Teo, but that's impossible. I need to know what happened to your mother."

"Se-cret!"

"Please, I need you to tell me."

"On-ly one per-son."

"Who?"

"My dad."

"It's me. I'm your dad. It's me, Ramiro."

No, Teo says with his face, "You're my grand-mother."

He takes pity on me, moving his arm out from under the sheet to hold my hand. The shrieks that reach us from the crack in the door tell us that September's kids have returned from school; Teo's grandchildren; my great-grandchildren.

4.1

SOMETIMES IT SEEMS LIKE I came out of flotation frozen; the need for light and heat comes from the need to recover my emotional system, which, for now, remains immobile. I want to shout at myself, give myself orders, shake off the icicles stuck in my hair and teeth.

I still haven't found my former best friend. I still haven't discovered what happened to my wife. I can't find any of her descendants. Teo doesn't recognize me. I feel useless in my own home. My desire to know drives me forward, but I get frustrated when my desire can't be fulfilled. To think that for decades I missed pain, and now that I'm back I'm incapable of feeling it.

I want someone to insult me on the street. But as I walk no one says anything. Some others drag batteries behind them, some eat ice cream in the plaza.

4.2

The real possibility of reincarnation hasn't meant we've achieved world peace. Before, it was verbalized more but now resentment is implicit. Everyone dedicates themselves to their passions and hates in silence; there isn't much left to report.

Public debate is focused on the use of bodies; a repetition of the debate over natural resources that had its heyday in the last century. Can a person be considered the owner of their body, even though other people will occupy it afterward? Bodily waste, although it's considered selfish, is not sanctioned except in extreme cases. The improvement and regeneration of organs contributes to the abuse. Procedures generate organic material that can perfectly imitate original parts and recreate specific functions. Thanks to these advances, the useful life of a body is extended, and many feel licensed to become even more irresponsible. Of course, given that the approval process for a body is costly, the debate is linked to the middle and upper classes. As a general rule, the greater the annual income, the less respect for a body. Millionaires setting fire to themselves bonzo style just to keep anyone from reusing their bodies seem to have created a tradition as esteemed as caviar.

Many vices that had been eradicated came back into fashion. The use of hard drugs is no longer condemned out of fear of danger to others, but for its damage to the body itself. The regeneration of lungs revived sales of cigarettes, which had nearly vanished; the prohibition of smoking in public spaces is still active but no longer enforced. It's often possible to distinguish people from my generation, whether they're in the body of a young or old person, by their aversion to tobacco.

The sustained furor for extreme sports got them officially added to the Olympic Games. The strict safety measures taken are merely a justification for including more shots of cadavers with their heads in line with their stomachs. Race car driving has abandoned all pretenses of safety precautions, drivers will sometimes use more than one body during the same championship.

Religion is still struggling to keep up. Just as it manages to reform itself, a new technology is invented that once again makes it obsolete. I sense a growing popularity in the Vedic doctrines as all major universities have a department of Eastern Studies. Of course, now, a country like Japan is full of Japanese with Western bodies.

After so much social turmoil, art has become more traditional and a respect for rules is valued above all else. Writers have new taboos to describe. Psychoanalysts invent new terminologies for old conflicts. Lawyers cash checks for tiny disputes over the application or non-application of the antiquated inheritance system. Doctors argue over whether it's ethical to allow the donation of the body of a particular person, or if bodies should be chosen at random. Political platforms promise to implement representation for the dead, or prioritize the living, depending on local tastes.

There are more and more supporters of the death penalty; criminals are burned into defective bodies. Executions are generally painful. I heard the story of a rapist who was electrocuted and then burned into a body with spina bifida. In another case, a serial killer was devoured, unanesthetized, by circus animals, with entrance free to the public; now he's in a section of the web that no one can access without a governmental password. The extension of life seems to have been accompanied by the extension of fascism.

4.3

To determine culpability for any eventual crimes related to bodily ownership the Koseki Register was established to record every change of body and the relationship that this creates to individuals. The Register helped to institutionalize family links that had been excluded from the legal system such as the relationship between a burned body and the parents of the original guest.

At first, anyone could access a copy of the Koseki of another person. Then a new law was implemented to limit access only to those who were authorized in that person's register. I asked to see my wife's register years ago but I was denied because I didn't appear on her list.

The Koseki allows for justice now that the body is an ambiguous piece of evidence, but it has also created many new forms of discrimination. With the right contacts, companies can use the Register to gather information on potential candidates; rich parents check the registers of their children's partners.

4.4

A woman in the body of a man dressed like a woman. A man burned into a new body rubs up against his sister until she asks for more. A nun commits suicide in order to be a priest in her new body. And sex always finds a way to reinvent itself despite limited positions and combinations.

It continues to be a powerful motivator: there's a pervasive drive to earn more money in order to buy a more attractive body. New tourist packages are sold, the most appropriate body included in the price. The lines are blurred between forbidden and permissible; hierarchies are reordered again and again. I know a man who wanted to name his child Bukkake, whether it was a boy or girl. Names are the first thing to adapt to new circumstances.

There is social pressure from groups trying to regulate sexual activity and they've seen a fairly large success rate among adolescents. One highly publicized movement lobbies for chastity as the most important societal value. The league prides itself in being made up of what they call authentic women. A journalistic investigation, however, revealed that at least two members of their directive committee had been, in their previous bodies, men.

In general, sex is more open than ever to the possibilities of the imagination. The internet is fertile ground for the circulation of rumors. The other day I heard that a man was euthanized in order to occupy the body of his wife who had died of an aneurysm. Then his wife was burned into her husband's body which sat waiting in a hospital freezer.

4.5

Technology isn't rational; with luck, it's a runaway horse, foaming at the mouth, ready to throw itself off a cliff in desperation. Our problem is that culture's tied to that horse.

At one time society's controversies were the printing press, medicine; today it's the state of flotation and the appropriation of bodies. Death still exists; what has disappeared is the certainty that everything will eventually end sooner or later. There's time to shave your head, time to let the gray hairs grow, to get pregnant, to torture, to be the world champion, and to rewrite the encyclopedia. With patience, a single person could build the pyramids; with perseverance, another single person could knock them down. I guess destruction is another form of love.

5.1

THE MAN WHO CLEANS THE HOUSE broke one of the computers. Teo's son got mad and fired him. I was out when it happened. When I returned it was like a bolt of lightning had fried any semblance of emotional equilibrium.

September is very angry; she says that they have to be patient with Cuzco, that it's not his fault that he's clumsy. Wales replies that Cuzco is a handicapped piece of shit and they don't have any business giving out charity, that's what the government is for. His wife says that she can do whatever she fucking pleases with her money, that she'll not only fix his computer but buy him a whole new one to download all the porn he wants. Meanwhile, I'm trying to hide behind the fruit basket, starving to death. I don't dare stand up, much less ask them to hand me a knife; I chew a green-gold pear, skin on, noiselessly, with sticky fingers.

Teo's bell interrupts them. "You can go," September shouts at him, "since you just fired the only person who took care of your dad." Wales huffs and puffs, opens the door to the refrigerator, slams it shut, and leaves the kitchen.

"The connection has been restored," says the cold voice of the fridge.

I'm resting the core of the pear in my palm when

September discovers me; her expression softens, I can almost see the muscles of her face surrender. Instead of speaking, she stretches out her hand so that I can give her the bare core. She opens the trash can with a stomp and throws it in without bending down.

I help her pick up the pieces of the computer, disemboweled across the living room. Bending over is uncomfortable for me so I sit down on the parquet floor. We start with the biggest pieces: carcass, internet cards, the monitor with its empty eye socket.

"They're getting more and more fragile," I tell her. "In my day they weren't exactly made of iron but they were more resistant. Computers were divided in parts and you had to connect them all together to make them work. My wife once unplugged the wrong cable and I'd lost everything. I got so mad that I ripped out all the other cables. I guess Wales inherited my temper." September doesn't smile.

The little pieces are hard to pick up. We sweep and sweep but they never make it into the dustpan. They seem to me to be made of clay or eggshell. The material is elastic, it molds the apparatus to the needs of the user, but the impact must have pushed it past its breaking point. September bites the tip of her index finger. I ask her for the broom and I start to remove the fragments stuck to the bristles. Every time I get a piece, I place it in the dustpan which September holds up.

"For a few weeks now we've been fighting about every little thing," she apologizes. "Please don't worry."

But I do: a few weeks ago is when I arrived. I realize that I'm sweating; walking around to clean up has worn me out.

When I finish, I hand the broom back to September. "I need to take a shower." I probably left the handle all sweaty.

"Oh," she says to me before I leave, "Vera was looking for you."

"Online?"

She remains silent: of course online. I thank her and continue on to the bathroom, although now I'd rather go straight to the computer.

5.2

I postpone the shower until after I visit the internet. I walk to my great-grandchildren's room, where the closest computer is located. The sound of shots announce the war game; I don't bother to knock. When I open the door I see my fat body bend in half on the huge screen; then I fall down. My body slaps the floor; my belly caves in; my tits go in different directions. "You hit the banana!" one soldier shouts to the other.

I brush my hair to the side so that I can see them: the boys are shielded behind an overturned chair. The floor seems to be covered in weeds, the same kind that grow in the garden outside September's office. In addition to the large screen, two computers orbit around vests that my great-grandsons are wearing. It's the first time I've seen this kind of computer. I only watched videos and read articles about them while I was in flotation. Technological advances are fueled by two necessities: conquering territory and entertaining children.

I gesture for the boys to come toward me. They take my arms without dropping their rifles; the computers float very close by. I manage to sit up; I don't want to fall down again. The shot that knocked me down left a hickey on my chest. I look at my arms and legs: bones and joints remain intact.

I shake the leaves from my dress.

"Doesn't anyone ever clean this room?"

"Cuzco!"

"I need to use one of the computers. I have to talk to great aunt Vera."

"What great aunt?"

"Aunt Vera."

"Oh yeah, Vera! She owes us our birthday presents!"

"But she's dead, boys."

"She can send them to us by internet!"

They squeeze me into one of the vests. It barely fits and I have to keep my elbows raised so that I don't strangle my armpits. The computer floats in front of me. I rest my fingers on the screen to advance to the node where I know I'll find Vera. The boys grab their heads: "You're so slow! Can't you go faster! This is boring!"

Vera is expecting me; she might have been waiting since she spoke to September, or even longer. A person on the internet can become Buddha, as long as they avoid the social networks and the pornography.

"Hi, Dad."

Her avatar is a flower.

"Oh, you've bloomed, the silence must be good for you."

"My brother on the other hand made very noisy fruits."

I say to Vera: "Wait a second while I find a quieter place."

She answers: "Tell the boys to look for their presents in the mail."

My great-grandsons celebrate by firing into the air. Just in case, I bend my head down and cover my chest with my hands. One of the boys gets hit in the back, but he doesn't fall down like I did; he just shakes for a few seconds and then curses his brother. It's the one who still has the vest on. Will I ever learn their names?

5.3

The computer orbits around me as I stand up; then it stops in front of me and follows me to the door. "It does everything but bark," I say to Vera, and the computer barks.

"I miss animal fur," she says. "When I was alive I only noticed the things I hated. Boiling water that blisters your skin. The rough walls I refused to touch. The stink of cows. Life is softer than I had always thought. Here, on the other hand, there's no roughness to caress. 'Flotation' is a good way to express it: there's nothing to grab onto."

"I never understood why they called it that."

"I do. It's named for the Japanese paintings of the floating world. A place where you only live in the moment, the moon, the snow, songs and fireworks, where everyone refuses to give into desperation or responsibilities. We float like gourds on the current of the stream."

"That's right, a Japanese invented it. I once knew someone who knew him."

"I know, Dad. I was there."

I'm in the doorway to the office in front of the empty patio. September rests her head on the desk, using her arms and clenched fists as a pillow. I sit on the bench outside; the computer lowers to the height of my fingers. I stop speaking and start typing:

"Your brother doesn't recognize me."

"Oh, Dad. Teo is old."

"We are too."

"You know it's different. I can't believe you! You're mad at him."

"No I'm not."

"Of course you are. But it's like being mad at a dog for peeing on the mattress or at the roots of a tree for breaking the sidewalk. Or at a battery for running out."

"He could do what we did."

"Even if Teo entered flotation, his mind is already drifting away. I'm sorry, but I'm not going to baby you. It's irreversible. There are wires in his mind that are just disconnected. I think he even prefers it that way."

"You speak to me like I'm not his father; like it doesn't hurt me."

"And how do you think we felt when you died?"

Vera disconnects, at least that's what it looks like, but I know she just went invisible. I feel like turning off the computer; better yet, like smashing it. It floats in front of me, unaware of its user's feelings. My daughter keeps writing invisibly.

"Everything falls apart eventually. Here inside we're deteriorating too. At some point the links are going to break, the data will be lost, and the lights are going to go out."

September comes out onto the patio with a pitcher in her hands. She bends down to water the plants, raising her dress to avoid staining it. The dirt absorbs the water instantly as steam rises from the scorched ground. With a gesture, she offers me some water and I accept. When I first sat down I was in the shade; now I'm in the sun.

"Stretch out your hands and I'll wet them for you."

"No, pour it on my head," I lean forward offering up the back of my neck. September brushes my hair aside, as if she were going to politely decapitate me. The freezing water ventilates the pores of my entire body. I throw my head back, clumps of hair matted together with water. The fat splashes on the ground last a blink and a half.

On the screen, Vera asks if I'm still there.

"I'm here," I write. September waves with her free hand as she returns to her office. I notice she's barefoot.

"Did you find your friend yet?"

"No."

"Are you still mad at him?"

"Yes."

"Wow. You've got to let go of that. It's not doing you any favors. Revenge is so out of fashion anyway. Find a new vice. No, wait! I have a brilliant idea: you could get married again. I'll plan the wedding. I can picture you in the most beautiful gown you've ever seen in your life. I might even rent a body for a day just to see that."

"And your mom, Vera, should we invite her too?"

"Don't be mean, I was just joking about the wedding. But I would like it. Mom is dead. Not like us. She's dead for real."

"Didn't you say we're going to die for real too some day? The system collapses, the screen goes blue, and then nothing."

"Yes, I think it's going to happen."

"Like Mom."

"And like Teo, when he dies of old age."

"Are you going to help me, Vera?"

"With what?"

"The same thing I asked you to help with when I was dead and you were alive. The same thing I asked you to do when we were both dead. What I'm asking you now that you're dead and I'm out here: I need to find your mom's children."

"You have me right here. And the other baby's in the house; he thinks you're his grandmother."

"The kids Mom had with her second husband."

I always try to avoid writing it out. I want to write it now, just to spit it out and expel the bad taste from my mouth: my wife's second husband, the man who married my wife and who fucked her, the husband of the widow.

"I didn't want to hide it from you, Dad. It was Mom who thought that distance and silence were the only solutions. And wasn't she right? You were always a vengeful ghost. Don't hate her for it, please."

"That hurts. I thought you knew me better than that."

"I know you love her more than anything in the world, that you always did, blah, blah, blah. I want to make sure you're not resentful. She just wanted to move on in the healthiest way possible. No one wants to go crazy at such a young age. What you say, that she was made for you, well she felt the same way about you. Oh, we hated you so much when you died."

"And that's why she got remarried."

"Well you could too. Now."

"I'm already dead. But there's a part of me that's still alive, and that's the part that needs to meet your mother's descendants. I can't find any record of them, but I know they're here. They're the ghosts, not me. I want them to be real. I want them to stop making me afraid."

"Okay, Dad, I get it. Mom's son and granddaughter live three blocks from the house. I'm sure you'll be able to find the place: it's covered in vines, the walls are painted yellow, it has a short fence with a little gate. You might have already walked by it."

"I walk by it every day. Is this a joke? So many years without knowing anything and now I can just walk over to see them?"

"Please don't scare the girl."

"You know her?"

"An adorable little girl. Send her my love; tell her she can visit me here, if she doesn't mind. It's easier for young people to connect than it is for us. Go. And please stop worrying about Teo. Spend some time with him. I would have loved to have a grandmother."

"Wait. September told me you were looking for me. What did you want to tell me?"

"Nothing, Dad. I just missed you."

"I miss you too."

":)"

Then she stops writing and I know that this time she's

really disconnected. I move my hands from the computer and I sit looking at the monitor until it goes black. I take off the vest and hang it on the back of the bench. The computer starts to rotate slowly around it; it looks like an owl during its daytime sleep.

5.4

I jog along with my battery hugged to my chest. When I walked to the end of the block for the first time, I needed help from Teo's grandkids; today each block seems so short. Almost immediately I'm in front of the house that Vera described, a place I've hardly even noticed.

The sun has dried up part of the vine, and the garden walls are an aggressive yellow color. The little elfin gate is closed but I step over it. Without struggling! It seems too good to be true that my knees finally respond to my commands. My fat heart vibrates, I feel it in the tips of my fingers. I rest my battery in front of the door. Before I ring the bell I decide it would be better to hide it behind me; I don't want to scare anyone. I press the doorbell but I don't hear it ring. I wonder if I should try again. All I can hear are the crickets complaining about the heat. I press the doorbell a second time; it doesn't make a sound.

"I heard you," someone shouts from inside. I flatten the wrinkles in my dress with my hands. A teenager opens the door. Her olive eyes match her tanned, bronze skin. She's just gotten out of bed, pillow marks still on her cheeks.

"You take a nap everyday too." As soon as I say it I realize how awkward it sounds and I want to bite into my fat fist. I ask her to let me in; I realize once again that I'm being rude. I laugh at myself and for a second I'm afraid that she's going to shut the door in my face. I don't know how to explain who I am; a long explanation is necessary for someone who probably thinks you're a door-to-door salesman. Of all the possible truths I choose the shortest: "I'm the person who loved your grandmother more than anyone." She may have hated her grandmother; or she might be one of those indifferent granddaughters that don't give a damn about their elders. Her eyes tell me that she loved her. Yes, I loved her too. She invites me in and offers me an iced tea. I'm so glad I don't wear diapers anymore.

5.5

Her name is Saffron and she's sixteen years old. On her arms that look naturally tanned she has blonde hair that looks artificially lightened. It's baby-fine, it stands on end for any reason: when she opens the refrigerator, when she takes ice out of the tray, when she leaves fingerprints on the pitcher fogged over with cold. She adds lemon to the tea. I imagine that she wouldn't have let me in if I'd been in my male body.

Wall hangings decorated with family trees line the living room. "It's a lost art form," she says very seriously. I look for my wife's name but I'm so nervous that I don't know where to start searching. Saffron sits on the couch, her bare feet resting on the upholstery. On her left leg I can see and hear an ankle bracelet, its jingling as hypnotic as a pendulum.

She asks me who I am. I don't want to tell her that I'm a man. Her eyes move to my battery resting on the floor next to me. I tell her that I was Adela's best friend (false) until I died when she only had her children with her first husband (true). Saffron quickly does the math: "Were you one of the first people in the country to enter flotation?" I tell her that I was (true). "Couldn't you talk to her from the web?" I tell her that we lost touch (true). "Why?" I tell her that Adela hated the internet (true). "But couldn't she have made the effort for you?" I tell her that I never felt resentment toward her for it (false). "Maybe she didn't love you as much as you loved her." I tell her that she loved me just as much as I loved her (impossible to prove).

I fall silent while Saffron arranges her skirt. "Don't be afraid to talk bad about my grandmother," she says. "I barely knew her." I'm ashamed to hear her speak about her ancestors with so little respect. Saffron explains the ins and outs of her life as I search for a resemblance to my wife. Her eyes, nose, and skin are all different but the shape of her neck is terrifyingly similar and her short hair allows me to admire it. She even scratches her ears with the same expression of disinterest in her surroundings.

The extracts of her biography can be summarized in the following way:

"I was born under Gemini, though I don't know if the Zodiac applies always or only in your original body. I still have my original body, but sometimes I fantasize about changing it for the body of an Asian girl. I like to chat with dead people and read the funny things old people search for on the internet. The cockroaches in my bedroom are my pets. When I was little I liked to read; now I prefer sports."

She finishes speaking and looks out the window and then at the clock. She stands up, anklet jingling, and says it might be better for me to go now. Her parents work all day and leave her home alone until nighttime. "You're welcome to come back," she tells me as she opens the miniature gate for me. "Next time I'll tell you about my grandma."

5.6

Cuzco arrives to the house at the same time as me, appearing just as I'm closing the door. I guess who he is because he shakes like I imagined he would. It's dark and he has bad breath; I'm not sure if I should let him in.

September turns on the light and suddenly I understand Wales's objections. Defining him as handicapped was not an insult, but a euphemism. Cuzco is a panchama: someone who died and returned to their original body. I'm shocked that September would hire him. When she's eager to get him quickly inside I realize that she doesn't want anyone in the neighborhood to know.

"No one saw you?"

"I waited until night to be secret, ma'am."

I think it's ridiculous that she's hired him to do housework; the panchama are clumsy, especially with their hands, it's like they've been reborn with carpal tunnel syndrome and they can't hold things properly. But I don't laugh: to annoy September would directly jeopardize my meals and my peace and quiet.

After dinner I take the shower I so badly needed. I can't take a bath because the tub is crowded with horse bones; Wales is a veterinarian. I'm careful with my cord; even in the shower I have to stay plugged in to my battery. And I remind myself that I can't fall asleep without remembering to charge it.

6.1

I REALIZE I NEED TO GET A JOB when I spend almost the entire day inside the house with a wet towel around my neck; when I find myself connecting again to the web, after I swore I wouldn't, to chat with the dead about events that occurred over fifty years ago; when I don't feel like going to bed at night but I also don't feel like getting up in the morning; and most of all, when September and Wales start to fight about me. They hide the reasons for their fights, but it's clear that the family is struggling to take care of me. I was never useless as a man, I'm not going to be useless as a woman.

Over breakfast I tell them that I'm going to look for a job.

Wales stares at me over his glasses that project his schedule for the day. "It's not easy to find work these days."

I smile and I can feel that it's a feminine smile. "That's what the news modules say."

September brushes my arm; her fingertips are sticky. "I think it's great that you want to get back into the workforce."

I look around for the jam but I don't see it. The kids bang their cups on the table. "We want to work too!" They have jam on their faces; September tries to scrub it off with a napkin. Wales offers me a piece of toast.

My hand shakes and the toast falls on the floor. I try to pick it up but it's hard for me to bend over. Cuzco appears with a rag. On hands and knees he wipes up the black jam with deep, slow movements. Wales had to give in to September's pleas to accept Cuzco back; but he can't even look at him. I tell Cuzco that I'll clean it up, to leave it, but he doesn't listen.

After breakfast I go up to my room and I pick out the prettiest dress I have in my closet. Most of them belonged to Vera; a few even belonged to my wife's mother. My breasts hurt just thinking about wearing them. I put on one of my mother-in-law's dresses with a flowered pattern that reminds me of Vera.

September shouts from the bottom of the stairs to ask if she can come up to help me. She still has her garden gloves on as she enters my room. "Sorry, sorry," I say, "I didn't mean to interrupt you."

"Don't be silly."

"I need help putting on my makeup," I confess. "I've never put on makeup in my life." I don't know why I tear up; it must be the hormones, or the heat.

September feels sorry for me, "Aww, my love!" she says, and she takes off her rough leather gloves. She sits me down on the lid of the toilet and closes the bathroom door.

"From bottom to top and then from top to bottom."

She makes me repeat it.

As she makes me up, she repeats the instructions from memory.

"First you put on your cream or lotion. Then concealer

on any spots or scars. Then comes your foundation, which has to be the same color as your skin or as similar as possible. You put it on with a sponge or with your fingers, make sure you don't forget the spots next to your ears and your neck. Powder over the foundation to set the makeup; it's translucent so your face won't be so shiny and it makes your foundation last longer. Now the eyes: first, shadow in the four strategic points of your eyelid; then you line your eyes and you put mascara on your lashes. Always touch your eyes with your ring finger only, the skin on your lower lid is very fragile and your index finger is too strong. Run a Q-tip over your eyebrows to remove any makeup that got stuck there, and you can brush them upward or whatever way you like. Brush some blush on your cheekbones. Last, you line your lips to give them shape, and then lipstick. You're a work of art. I should take a picture of you or freeze you just like this."

I thank her, tell her how much it makes my eyes stand out; I don't want to tell her that it looks like I stuck my face in a birthday cake, or that I'm afraid that chunks of cream are going to fall to the floor when I move. I force myself to look in the mirror and admire September's neatness and delicacy. I'd tell her so if only I could breathe.

I get up from the toilet and the makeup doesn't fall off of my face. I move my head from side to side, I smile, I make faces, and everything stays in place. I give September a kiss on the cheek. She puts her gloves back on and she hooks her arm in mine. As we walk down the stairs together I feel like I'm reliving the sweet sixteen I never had.

6.2

The taxi driver asks me what palace I'm going to looking so pretty. It must be the makeup; I have to remember to tell September. She lent me her cell phone in case I need to call, but I don't even know how to turn it on.

It's the first time I've been downtown in almost a hundred years. The number means nothing to me. The taxi driver tries to chat with me but his words fade into the urban landscape. I see buildings that aren't there anymore in my mind like a tracing superimposed over reality. I assimilate the new constructions; I've seen a lot of them in the online maps. Sixty hours of new images as I snorkeled through the streets and subways in virtual reproductions that include everything, even the filth. Maps are the literature of the future. Maps and urban landscape, fused into one fluid, permeable substance. Tastes change, art endures in the artifacts: an ancient water fountain, a door, a bus shelter.

The heat is thick as I get out of the taxi. A woman asks me where I bought my dress. I explain that I inherited it. "Thanks," she says with a smile as she walks away. I watch her then ring the bell. A voice asks who I am.

"Ramiro Olivaires."

The plaque on the building reads: "Graciano, Olivaires, Lavalleja, Architects."

They let me in.

A receptionist asks what she can do for me. I ask to speak with the architects. She closes her eyes before answering: "I don't think they're available at the moment."

I try to be friendly: "I can wait."

She makes a call. While I wait, I watch as a series of last spring's trends pass across the surface of the coffee table. The themes cycle through, a tropical aesthetic in greens and blues with a clear influence from Indian design.

When I raise my head the secretary is watching me.

I smile at her and I make a sweeping wave of my hand. "I founded this studio almost a century ago."

"Yeah," she responds.

"Before, this was a plastic surgeon's office. Back then it was a market directed at the rich, not like now. We bought it from a surgeon who ripped his customers off. He injected them with cement."

The secretary answers the phone. She nods her head several times; I don't know who's on the other end of the line.

She hangs up and remains silent for a moment, her head bowed in an unending prayer.

"Ma'am . . . sir. I'm sorry but you're going to have to leave."

"I'll be brief. I won't bother them at all. With my experience I could be of significant help in certain matters that they haven't even considered. A five-minute meeting, that's all I'm asking for."

"They say they don't care."

"Please. I was their grandfathers' partner."

"They say they don't care about that either."

"I see."

I feel my forehead flood with sweat.

"Would you like me to bring you a glass of water?"

"Yes," I respond.

She searches for a glass in the drawers of her desk; she wipes it off with her finger and then blows in it. When she brings it back full of water from the dispenser I can see her fingerprint on the glass. The cold water stings my throat but I don't stop until I've drunk it all. I wipe my mouth with my palm and it comes away covered in makeup. I rub my hand on my dress, leaving a stain. I hand the glass back to the secretary and I have the urge to ask for a napkin to wipe my dirty fingerprints off of it.

Next to the door, I use September's phone to scratch what remains of my name from the plaque outside.

6.3

Three more attempts to find work end in disaster as I don't meet the conditions they require for the particular position; at least that's their excuse.

The first is a tea house; I'm "too young."

The second is a butcher's shop; I'm "too old."

The third is a sports complex; I'm "too ladylike." They say that maybe if I return in another body I could make it to the next stage in the interview. They give me a telephone number in case I decide to have the operation.

In the three cases I'm "too fat" but they don't tell me that. I'm never going to complain about my body again. Even if my knees give out and my tits swell up like they're frozen inside.

6.4

I stay away from the yellow house with the little gate until I feel capable of talking about my defeat without wanting to vomit. I spend a week dozing between the sheets and the soapy water in the tub, surrounded by the smell of the scorched patio. For the first time since I left flotation I have no appetite.

"You should be eating much more now," September protests. "Sucking on apricots and spitting out the seeds isn't going to help you get stronger."

I put on makeup again to visit Saffron. I do it all on my own, much more simply than the previous time. September gives me her approval even though she doesn't know where I'm going.

"Wait," she says, and she brings me a hair clip in the shape of a curled up cat. As I tuck it in to my hair I imagine my head as a comfy cushion for the cat and the thought makes me smile.

There's a breeze outside but it's hot and stuffy inside the house. I swing open the screen door as I leave. Wales has proclaimed war on the mosquitoes, leaving the walls stained with blood and tiny exoskeletons.

I don't get too sweaty since it's just a few blocks to the yellow house. I'm the only one out on the street. The branches of the trees are overcrowded with green and the sidewalks too. Saffron is outside smoking a cigarette; the smoke scares the mosquitoes away. Her skirt is pulled up to her knees. The ankle bracelet isn't on the same leg as last time.

"Is it true that the dead feel the heat worse than the living?"

I tell her that I'd never heard that as I sit down next to her.

"They say the dead have to take baths in tubs full of ice. Like people who survive being struck by lightning. They overheat like the old computers used to. Maybe because inside they're all full of dust."

"I'm not full of dust inside," I laugh. "I have lungs, a pancreas, and a heart. I think the only thing I'm missing is a kidney."

"You're not sure? Did they steal it while you were sleeping, or what?"

"This body didn't come with everything. It's all my family could afford with the budget they had. It works, and that's all that matters."

"You don't miss your old body?"

"I don't think so. I've never thought about it but I don't think so." I picture my erect ghost member. "Just certain details."

"And were you pretty before?"

I should have told her upfront that I was a man but I lied the first time and now it's too late: the deception stuck fast and I can't unstick it without also undoing the truth.

"Yes, I was very pretty."

Of course that was the wrong answer. The beautiful and the hideous require elaboration and precise words; only the mediocre is brushed aside. I curse my narcissistic desire to impress her even with my lies.

"What did you look like? Do you have a picture?"

"Oh, no," I simulate an unexpected modesty.

"I can search for you on the web."

"I was a redhead, honey-colored eyes, tall but with delicate hands."

I think I'm describing my girlfriend from high school. Adela hated her with such passion that she made me describe her so that she could meticulously criticize every aspect of her. The small hands distorted into circus freak show dwarf hands, her small waist featured a disgusting belly button, her shiny copper hair became an omen of bad fortune, her smell attracted dogs, and flies sprouted from her breath. The most important part of the ritual was that Adela needed to hear it from my mouth. Aside from this one fixation Adela was a sweet and generous girl. She actually got along well with the rest of my ex-girlfriends.

Saffron frames my current body with her fingers. I adopt the expression of a model on a catwalk. Then she confesses: "I wouldn't like to be fat if I had been skinny before."

I want to tell her that getting fat or drying up as you age is inevitable, you never stay like you were when you were young. Young people today have no reason to fear old age. I wonder what happens to the bodies of the elderly when the government decides they aren't ready to be cremated but nobody wants to buy them. There's always a desperate case, but in general disgust is stronger than desperation.

"I don't mind," I answer. I'm telling the truth. There's something about this short old lady that's endearing to me and it means much more to me than my previous skinny but defective body. "Are you going to tell me about your grandmother?"

"Yes, of course, later. First I wanted to ask you

something, well, I'm embarrassed."

Just as I was about to lose my patience, Saffron leaned her head forward to expose her flexible bronzed neck.

"Whatever you want. Ask me whatever you want."

"What was it like to die?"

She looks at me innocently with her olive eyes and I understand that it's a ploy. She wants to soften me up with her glance, to coax me into talking about something that she knows I don't want to explain. Death is the real deal, something that can't be faked, the slippery, heavy thing that's constantly in view even though no one can describe it. In order to enter into flotation you have to die. There are no express trains that skip a few stations, no sleeper car where the passenger can take a nap and wake up later in a new fish bowl. Computers can't simulate it. Artists can't recreate it. It's my death and no one else's. I can't even articulate my negative response the way I'd like to.

"Death is secret, universal, and obligatory."

Saffron grabs my arm. Instead of moving away I pull her closer. She squeezes me. Physical contact is a relief when I'm thinking too much. I would like to stay still and enjoy her morbid fascination, but I decide to stand up and leave.

"Don't go."

"You promised you'd tell me about your grandmother and you're not doing it."

I hate that everything feels like a game, I hate that she is sixteen, beautiful, and descends from the love of my wife and another man.

"I'm going to tell you if you would just come back and sit down with me. I just didn't want you to leave after I told you. It's too short."

I'm glad it's short; long stories get their hooks into you and it's hard to get free of them. I sit back down.

"My grandmother always seemed like a quiet person to me, so I never imagined too much about her life. Just, you know, the normal: everyone has some secret that sets them apart from everyone else. It's just that sometimes a secret can destroy a person. My dad didn't find out that my grandma had another family until several years ago. I was little but I remember. Dad cried and he couldn't understand how it was possible that Grandma Adela had had two families. It was so unbelievable, like having two heads or two hearts. It turns out my aunt not only knew; she had grown up with the kids of my grandma's first marriage. When Dad was a baby, those kids were already grown and they had a fight with their stepdad, my grandfather. They decided not to tell Dad anything, even after my grandma had died. You already know that she didn't want to enter flotation and she died definitively. After Dad found out, he met Grandma's mysterious children. Aunt Vera and Uncle Teo. Vera is in flotation, you would love her. Teo lives four blocks away from here, but he's really strange. I'm a little bit afraid of him. Because of all this I started dabbling in genealogy. If my dad had studied the family like me he would have found out sooner about your friend Adela's secret."

It's not such a short story but I still have a few questions. Saffron answers them as best she can. It's hard to assimilate and hard to express with words that don't allow for ambiguities. I keep thinking about Saffron's grandfather, who didn't want the two families to be in contact: he must have thought that it would save them all the pain. I think about Adela, who didn't want to talk to me ever again: I was her dead and she had to get rid of me in order to move on. It's just that I can't get rid of her, and I don't have anywhere to move on to. I suppose that she was wiser than me; it wouldn't be the first time, although it was the last.

I promise Saffron that I'm going to come back to tell her about when they first invented flotation and the dead started occupying the first burned bodies. These things really fascinate her. As I walk back home, I realize that Saffron is an exact copy of the models I saw in the fashion modules, but she pulls it off. At night, I masturbate using as a tutorial a porn video in which two drunk girls kiss each other in the shower. Having an orgasm on a foreign body is more complicated than you'd imagine.

7.1

IN THE TOY AISLE AT THE PET SHOP Wales tries to console me over my employment failure; he seems worried. He reminds me that there are agencies that help the burned reinsert themselves into society. With a rubber puppy in my hand, I promise to give it a shot. I hate being useless and I hate being a bad grandfather even more.

I know what's in store for me with one of these agencies: the majority of the burned who carry batteries go to work for the state. I feel like a charity case. When we return home I sit on the couch, I experience a throbbing pain after the smallest effort. Cuzco is on all fours, cleaning the patio tiles; the kids got paint all over them. The direct sun of midday still hasn't hit the yard, but he must be hot. I ask him if he wants a glass of water. He tells me no and thanks, without raising his head, a few feet from the ground.

The first weeks, Cuzco wouldn't even talk to me. I tried to loosen him up every day with questions and assistance in his daily tasks. His face remained expressionless even when he fumbled. He responded for the first time when I asked him if he had a family. At that moment, Cuzco was putting away the dinner plates. September watched him from a chair in the kitchen: a broken dish would mean another fight with Wales. When Cuzco couldn't wipe any more spots off the plate he had in his hands he finally answered that yes, he had a beautiful family.

"Very sweet kids and a little dog that never stops barking at me, ma'am."

Since then Cuzco usually answers me when I talk to him. I find myself wondering about him a lot. I know he leaves on Fridays at midnight and returns Monday early in the morning. No one, not even September, knows where he goes. "If he goes to stay with his family," I gossip, "why does he always return so dirty?" Cuzco has his own shower next to his bedroom; the first thing he does Monday morning is take a long shower. September always has a fresh change of clothes for him in a drawer in the bathroom.

He compensates for his clumsiness with a meticulous attention to detail; maybe that's why September defends him. Kneeling in the patio, as the sun begins to make the tiles shine, Cuzco looks like a priest giving mass.

7.2

I need Wales to help me unbuckle my seat belt so that I can breathe. I squirm in this slippery body, full of flesh, which gave me shelter and accepted me as a guest when no one else would. My grandson offered to drive me to the employment agency. On the way we talk about soccer. "The famous players never retire," he tells me. "They can keep going on sheer willpower, mind over body." I say I agree but I don't think I do.

Before getting out of the car, I ask him if he knows anything about phantom member syndrome; I don't mention my penis. Wales tells me he remembers too little from veterinary school to be able to help me. "The medical text that deals with that syndrome is called *Phantoms in the Brain*, written by an Indian man." I think it's probably the best definition I've ever heard to explain the soul: a ghost in the brain. I get out of the car and I thank him.

The agency is in an outlying neighborhood. The building it's housed in must be from my time; I might have even designed it, but I don't see my name on the front. A girl in the doorway asks me for spare change; she's either pregnant or she has a huge tumor in her stomach. Before Wales drives away he reminds me that I can call him at the vet's office when I finish. The kids taught me how to use this kind of cell phone; luckily there's no self-destruct button.

The other applicants are worse off than I am; in some cases you can tell there was a glitch in the burning process. The elderly bodies I haven't seen anywhere else are all here. Some of these decrepit forms must host young minds who were unable to obtain a more suitable site for reincarnation. It's better to be dead, I tell myself, gripping the rail.

A conveyor belt lined with chairs runs through the middle of the office; I sit in the closest seat. Invisible employees seem to be controlling the time spent at each stop, we're moved between stations at regular intervals, unless one of the burned takes too long in their response. At the first stop, a voice asks me for my date of birth and my date of death, my identification number and my reincarnation number. At the second stop, my birth sex and my chosen sex; at the third stop, they ask me what kind of experience I have and what kind of work I'm looking for. At the fourth stop, they offer me a hot tea made from herbs I've never heard of; at the fifth stop, they photograph me, front and back. To reach the sixth stop my seat veers off into a waiting area; the seventh and final stop is outside of my line of vision.

My illusions of grandeur where discarded into the basket of the pregnant girl at the door. When the voices asked me what kind of job I was looking for, I responded that anything was fine. Maybe working outside would help me to be healthier; but in reality, my muscles probably wouldn't be able to support the weight and the humidity. I leave to the state the responsibility of deciding my future, unless they plan for me to remain unemployed. The right not to work is new and is now considered the most fundamental of human rights; but the idea turns my borrowed stomach.

I realize that the wait is taking a long time when they offer me a second cup of tea; the worker, a bearded teenager, asks me how I take it. I ask for sugar, maybe the riskiest thing I've done since I left flotation. I immediately feel guilty for damaging this body that my family worked so hard to get for me.

I still haven't decided whether or not I would finish the tea when a man in sports clothes extends his had to me: it's very hairy. He helps me stand. Then he opens the door to the closest office and gestures for me to enter. "Sorry, I've just arrived." He straightens his glasses as I sit and then he does the same. Almost no one uses glasses anymore, except the computerized kind with screens in the lenses; his look like they're just glass. He moves some objects around on the desk and introduces himself as Moses. In his left hand he holds a slip of paper with a government seal.

"Are you really one of the first people in the country to have gone into flotation? It's fascinating. I hope you won't mind if I ask you a few questions."

The man must know Saffron. He asks every imaginable question: dates, relatives, locations, connections, procedures, interventions, machines, internet usage. Every response generates at least three new questions. When he finally runs out of things to say, I ask him what kind of job he has in mind for me; his questions only managed to confuse me.

Moses raises his bushy eyebrows. "I thought they'd told you. I'm a cybernetic archeologist."

"And what are you doing working here?"

"I don't! They called me over because of you. This isn't my office. Do you see any photos of my grandkids? Believe me, my office is much more elegant. But we weren't going to make you walk more than you needed to with that battery you're carrying around."

I would like to thank him but I'm too embarrassed about my battery to say anything. "I'd like to not have to use it anymore," I confess. "Every day I feel like it weighs twice as much as the day before."

"I think we can probably come up with a solution . . . if you come work for us."

"I have no idea what a cybernetic archeologist does. I've heard the term but that's it. I don't know how I could be qualified for that job."

"You're afraid you're an impostor. Don't be afraid. The life experience you've had makes you more than qualified. Think of it this way: how could a real, live ancient Sumerian artisan aid the work of an archeologist? Internet modified reality by turning it into an object; the web has an existence as concrete as the cities of any civilization. The present is superimposed on the past so the regular user can only access the top layer of the web, but we know that each version created a new layer. We're most interested in what was deleted: the deleted articles of Wikipedia are more important than the ones that weren't: why would an article have been erased from an encyclopedia that proposed to include everything? The things that were made to disappear hold the key to humanity. Our job is to dig down and reconstruct what has been destroyed, replace what has been lost, bring the invisible to light before it disappears for good. It's too much work to do on our own; think of the digital storage units as boxes full of artifacts: megabytes, gigabytes, and my favorite: terabytes. Did you know that *tera* meant *monster* in Greek? The internet is my personal Tyrannosaurus Rex; if the web were a living thing, we'd call it cybernetic paleontology. I'm content to call it archeology. It's as hard as it is rewarding: systems transform, conventions change, the web is built over unstable swampland. Some objects are absorbed and others expelled. I'll be able to ask you questions using what, for most people, is specialized jargon. Can you tell me the difference between a Betamax and a VHS? What sound did the first modems make? Can you explain what exactly a .gif was? Your face tells me you can! Excuse my overenthusiasm. You're my Sumerian artisan."

I ask Moses why he needs me; I wasn't the only one around then and I'm not the only one who's still around now.

"Do you know how hard it is to find you guys? There were no records kept at first. The Koseki Register wasn't implemented until years after your death. Stop worrying and just accept the job."

We shake hands and I stand up. Moses asks me shyly if I'm any relation to September. He must have recognized her married surname was the same as mine. I tell him yes, that she's the wife of my grandson. He smiles broadly. "She's a very well-respected researcher," he informs me. His enthusiasm is catching when he makes me promise to send his regards.

As I turn to go, Moses raises his hairy hand. "I'm legally obligated to ask you one more thing. At the agency we prioritize the integration of other connections from your past life. Due to the antiquity of your case we could make due with someone who was a child when you died. If there's someone you'd like to recommend, they could also join our office." He looks around for something that he can't seem to locate. Finally he googles its coordinates and discovers what he was searching for beneath the polaroid camera that he brought in with him, covered in a clear protective film. He hands me an electronic tablet and asks me to point out my contacts from my past life. The catalogue is an extensive database that includes names, addresses, and telephone numbers. I instinctively search for the name of my former best friend. It pops up immediately: he entered flotation seven years after I did. He now uses the body of a one-eyed man. He lives an hour and a half from my house.

7.3

I return home by taxi so that I don't have to bother my grandson again; he's treating a giraffe today, not in a zoo but at the home of a private citizen. I find the house empty except for Teo, in his bed like always. I give him my good news; I force myself to stop thinking about my friend.

Teo nods and smiles. I squeeze both his hands as we talk: they're not as cold as they were before. I tell him about my new job, about Moses, about the money I'll be making. "What do you think of the good news?" I ask him. "They're my pres-ents," he tells me. We're both happy: me to be able to spend time with my son; him, to be with his grandma. We're interrupted by shouts from beyond the hall. Teo starts to cry. I tell him not to worry, that it's probably the television. He covers his head with the sheet; through the thin fabric I can see his mouth hanging open, like a ghost of the new century.

I close the door and walk silently to the kitchen. Wales is sitting on the floor, against the wall. September is breaking all the dishes in the house. The voice of the kitchen computer announces how many plates remain as she shatters them against the floor: "Five soup bowls." They are both crying and shouting nasty insults at each other, words that begin to rot before they are even pronounced. "Four soup bowls." Moses's kind regards will have to be relayed at another moment. "Three soup bowls."

8.1

I'm woken up by the pain of an elephant-sized erection. My phantom member feels like it broke off as I slept. The body I inhabit never stops surprising me; I thought it would be fascinating to have a vagina, but my mouth is the orifice I am most preoccupied with. I could dunk my whole arm in cream and lick and gnaw it to the bone. I have a weakness for meat. To obtain a kilo of tenderloin, cows are no longer necessary; their cells are placed in a petri dish and the meat is grown from there. Even some vegetarians accept this kind of meat. My body is large because of someone else's indulgences but I have to eat to match my size which makes me happy.

The changes in my appetite must have been brought on by the replacement of my old battery for a more modern version. The new one is wireless; the old one is now just more junk taking up space in the downstairs bathroom. I had to have surgery to install the new device. I went back to the hospital for the first time since I left flotation, but I wasn't scared: September went with me. I was only there for a few hours; I imagine what I felt was similar to a well-executed abortion. Now I carry the new battery in a backpack, and it's strong enough that I can leave it beside my desk while I'm at work. I still have to charge it every night, but at least I can shower without being attached to a cable like a harpooned whale.

I got the wireless battery thanks to Moses. We've developed a respectful relationship that never goes beyond work-related topics; the only exception is when he asks about September. I can't bring myself to tell him that she's about to divorce my grandson for reasons unknown to me.

The kids have no idea either; the noise from their room drowns out their parents' quiet but constant erosion. The last time I went into their playroom it had been converted into a desert scene from an old cowboy and Indian movie. They played at killing me for being a cowboy deserter; the sand stuck under my fingernails as I lay on the ground. I didn't say a word, I just closed my eyes until they stopped shooting me.

8.2

"How does the black market work now?" I ask Moses during a break. I keep thinking about my former best friend when I'm at the office, when I'm in the toilet, and when I can't sleep at night. Moses listens patiently to what I tell him and explains patiently when I have questions.

"The body market?"

He looks at me through his glasses that don't do anything at all.

"Yes," I respond.

"Unregistered bodies. Illegal surgeries. One-day rentals. Minors. Teams of disposable bodies for extreme sports. Guerillas. Chemical experiments. Clitorises the size of a thumb, if that's what you're into."

"How do they get away with it?"

"Well, there are psychologists and forensic analysts who can determine if a person is who they say they are. Linguistic experts and computer technicians are very useful as well. But in general to be able to trace a contraband body you need some kind of clue to start with. Are you thinking about committing a crime?"

"I was thinking of killing someone."

"To change bodies?"

"For revenge."

"Does this person like their body a lot?"

"He's ugly and he's missing an eye."

"Well then killing him would be doing him a favor. If he's the victim of a murder the state will offer him a better body as compensation."

I remain silent and Moses takes the opportunity to ask me about the exchange of passwords as proof of love when I was young. He scratches his beard with his hairy hand. Whatever I say is immediately recorded in the computer that follows Moses around everywhere; he sometimes even takes it when he goes jogging.

8.3

Despite my new income I still live with my family: I want to stay close to Teo, but I also still need assistance. Cuzco helps me even though they don't pay him extra to do it. In some twisted way I'm happy about it: the absence of payment allows me to feel that I'm assisted not by an employee, but by a friend.

They say that the panchamas have different blood and bones from the rest of us, that they have bigger cocks or that they're animals; some refer to them as "four-fingered" or "four-legged beasts." The Koseki Register flags them in job interviews and they end up with the work no one else wants to do. They live in the least hygienic places and the media completely ignores them except to blame them for the unemployment rate. People who think that way must have been burned with hearts of stone; they don't know Cuzco, and they don't want to. He's polite and efficient, quiet but friendly, loyal to the last vertebrae. Some argue that the law of nature dictates that you must change bodies after death; it seems that one prejudice only disappears once another arises to replace it. September agrees with me, but she's not willing to publicly admit that she's hired a panchama.

8.4

I sit on the couch in the dark watching Cuzco. He's finishing up with the dinner plates; at midnight he'll leave to spend the weekend at home. Little bugs stick to the light in the kitchen. The family is asleep.

Cuzco stops working as soon as the kitchen clock marks midnight. He washes his hands and dries them on a towel. When he finishes he hangs it on the oven door. He goes to his room to get a khaki colored bag, sets the alarm, and leaves the house through the back door. I get up off the couch and deactivate the alarm so I can follow him.

The treetops join up in the middle of the street; pollen drifts down like snow. Cuzco moves away on foot and I follow him for fifteen blocks to the train station. We wait for five minutes: he's next to the yellow line and I'm hidden behind a rusted-out old newspaper stand. It's the last train of the day. I sit next to the window several seats behind Cuzco; checking to make sure he's still seated at each station. A woman blocks my view from time to time and I have to crane my neck to see him. Many of the passengers struggle to keep their heads up from exhaustion or fall fast asleep with their mouths wide open. The only ones awake are the groups of rowdy passengers making jokes.

As the stations pass only the ugliest passengers remain. When we get to the last station we all get off: a blind couple holding hands, a woman with her face eaten up by disease, a man with the arm of a three-year-old boy, Cuzco, another panchama that walks without raising his eyes from the ground, and this sweaty fat lady. There are no signs that tell me so, but I know we're near Gorila.

The blind couple, Cuzco, the other panchama, and me, in that order, cross a narrow piss-soaked bridge over a

drainage ditch. There must be other entrances to the shantytown but this is surely the most poorly lighted, which
is all the better for me. I follow Cuzco more closely. The
panchama that stares at the ground smells like seafood. The
entrance to the shantytown is muddy. Despite the fact that
it's past midnight, the distant murmur becomes a hundred
people in crumbling, damaged bodies, shopping and stroll-
ing the alleyways of the former cemetery.

Strips of sheet metal cover the walkways hung with
numerous lightbulbs, Gorila is brighter by night than by
day. The narrow paths and empty spaces between the mau-
soleums are too narrow and irregular for patrol cars or
ambulances to pass through. Merchandise must be brought
in over the roof marked with large holes where the metal
has rusted away from the droppings of birds and bats.
Goods are lowered in to fill up the ten thousand claustro-
phobic stalls. The gravestones and crosses were immediately
weeded out and the few that remain are considered bad
luck; no one wants to break them because that would be
worse luck still. The houses are made of wood and metal,
makeshift shelters of cardboard and fabric, upended dump-
sters. Egg stands are housed in crypts, the butcher shop is
next to the cremation oven, the only part of the old cemetery that still functions. The people of this shantytown
don't appear in the Koseki Register. The news modules
repeat that Gorila is the only place in the city without
internet access, those of us who were in flotation know it's
not true, they just have a less stable connection. I guess
poor people also need to talk to their dead.

"I catch you looking at my son and I'll break your head

open," a woman says to me. To her left, a five-year-old boy is tied to a post.

Cuzco moves rapidly through the maze of the former cemetery and my back is already in pain. I had resolved never to complain about this body, but the pain is too sharp; maybe it's the weight of the backpack. The smell of chlorine assaults my nostrils. Cuzco ducks into a house as quickly as he left mine: unceremoniously and without hesitation.

The wooden house has been built above a family crypt that must have been luxurious when it was constructed; its former splendor is reflected in the moldings. The door is tied closed with a cable, and inside clothes hang where the coffins once stood. Along the wrought-iron gate around the vault, the cement tiles are broken; vegetables grow out of the holes. The upper building is accessed by a rope ladder; I'm surprised that Cuzco, with his clumsiness, was able to climb up so quickly.

I don't dare pass through the gate and I doubt the rope ladder would hold my weight. I stand in front of the house. A dog barks from the top floor. I hide behind a fruit stand across from the crypt. Little green flies surround me. Cuzco comes back out through the gate and walks away down the narrow alley. I scare the flies away and follow him.

I squeeze between vendors of toy machine guns, discarded computer parts, pets curled up next to the light poles. I wanted to see where Cuzco lived and I did; I don't know where he might be going now. I want to call out to him so he'll stop and invite him to have a drink in the bar that takes up part of the street, but I wouldn't know how

to explain why I'm in Gorila. I swear to myself that I'm not
going to let him go without talking to him.

8.5

I lose track of Cuzco when I see my former best friend dis-
playing the contents of a little portable freezer to a group
of prospective customers. My muscles stiffen but the other
pedestrians push me toward him as they squeeze past.

Bragueta looks at me with the one eye of his new body
and confuses my shock for the interest of a possible cus-
tomer. I have no doubt that it's him. He not only matches
the photo in the Register, but also has the same manner-
isms: he flattens his hair down with one hand, he pounces
on anyone who will pay attention to him. I wish I had
strong muscles so that I could burst open the one good eye
he has left, but my weak old lady arms don't even respond.

He shows me the contents of the freezer: low-quality
organs. A lung inflates and deflates like the paper sack of
a paint huffer.

"Wholesale prices, ma'am, tell me what you need and
I'm sure I'll have it," he says to me.

It's the first time I've seen Bragueta in over half a century; I never thought that when I found him I'd be in this
body with fat tits. I hated him so much and he's not even
able to recognize me. I grab him by the clothes. "It's me,"
I tell him.

"Who?"

"Me!"

The group around us breaks up and leaves us alone. My back is sweating and one of the straps of my backpack slides off my shoulder. Everything is sweaty: my hands, the crypts, the trash, the entire shantytown sweats.

Bragueta looks me in the eyes, his mouth hanging open. "I remember," he says, and I let him go. He straightens his clothes. He closes the door of the freezer and picks it up in one hand; it must be lighter than it looks.

"We have to talk," I tell him.

With his free hand, Bragueta rips my battery off my back and takes off running. I'm pulled toward him and then I fall to the ground. I scrape my hand against the broken cement tiles. I stand up as fast as I can: too slowly. Bragueta is disappearing into a side alley, his freezer and my backpack swinging in his hands. He slides easily between the stalls as everything becomes an obstacle for my cumbersome body. I can barely make him out in the crowd. I slip on a synthetic heart: it must have fallen from his freezer. One of my shoes comes off. My former friend is nowhere to be seen.

I'm lost in the maze of Gorila without the battery I need to live. My urge to shit is too strong for me to try and make it to a bathroom. I defecate myself but I'm no longer wearing diapers like when I first left flotation. The shit slides down my thighs to my knees.

I don't know where to go. I don't even know how to stand.

I no longer have control of my body. I scream desperately for a battery; everyone stares at me but no one understands. A couple of women laugh at the stain which now extends down to my feet. I sit in the middle of the alley and my body blocks the way completely. Someone is shaking me but I can't bring myself to look at them. I feel squeezed tight in this body as if it can no longer contain me.

A woman with a megaphone touts the benefits of religion. I smell smoke as panic begins to overcome my humiliation. I crawl on all fours until I reach a post I can grab onto to stand up. Halfway up the pole my arm detaches from my body. I manage to remain upright. Bare bone is exposed down to my elbow and the flesh of my forearm lies on the ground like a discarded glove.

My eyelids are heavy; I take a few steps to the only corner of Gorila it seems the artificial light doesn't reach. My stomach bursts open like a piñata. I hold my intestines up with the only arm I have left. I'm standing on a tombstone that I refuse to fall down on top of. My legs shake, I think they're about to fall off like my arm did. As I collapse I notice that the ground is filthy.

Old and mangled bodies stare down at me. I want to say something to them, but I don't know what. My intestines are slippery as I try to keep them from unraveling.

9.1

I HAVE NO IDEA HOW they got me out of Gorila; I just know that I was in flotation again. The body I had died; I guess the panchamas had to sweep up the rotten remains of her stuck to the ground. Or maybe some dog ate them. I'm in another body now and I feel sharp pains all over. The good news keeps coming in. The doctors just let me know that my body is so young and healthy that I'm not going to need a battery for a while. I'm also going to be able to leave the hospital soon. But the best part is that I'm no longer suffering from phantom limb syndrome in my groin: the flesh has been restored. They burned me into the generous body of an African man. My palms are white and my lips are meaty.

My family could never have afforded such a body; the acquisition is thanks to Moses's contacts. I feel like getting up and running, but I still have to stay in bed. I feel like I'll never sleep again and I have a voracious appetite. But the good times, when I could eat whatever I wanted, are over for now; I have to take good care of this magnificent lacquered body. When the lights go out in my room I miss my adorable fat old lady.

9.2

They load me into an ambulance like a half-frozen side of beef. My family follows behind in their car. As they position me in my wheelchair and roll me toward the house I hear September criticizing Wales's driving. Wales complains about the way the nurses are handling me. The boys shout insults at pedestrians and then duck behind the car. Home at last.

I wait for Wales to leave for work then I ask September how they found me. "It was Cuzco who saved you," she tells me proudly. "He plugged you in to a battery until the medics could get there, but they took too long and the putrefaction was irreversible."

I stand in the back doorway holding on to the top of the frame. I like being tall and feeling the sun spill onto my long back.

"What were you doing in Gorila, Rama?"

I explain who I was following and who I ran into. September is honest and a good listener, but I don't want to talk. I know that later on, when I can't fall asleep and I'm kicking at the sheets until they fall off of me, I'm going to regret my secrecy. But September doesn't ask me about Bragueta, like I assumed she would, but about Cuzco. At first I think it's because she's grateful to him; then she tells me that because of the accident the neighbors found out about him and they asked Wales to fire him.

"So it's too late. He saved me and then you guys fired him."

"Of course we didn't. Not only because I'm opposed. For some reason, Wales defends him now."

It's not likely that Wales feels grateful to Cuzco. I try to imagine his reasons but none seem to fit with my grandson's personality and I don't dare ask September if it was because of a fight they had. We sit in silence for a moment and she runs her index finger over my bicep; her touch feels electric.

"I'm amazed by your new body," she confesses.

I try to change the subject.

"Where is Cuzco now?"

Her finger falls away.

"Giving Teo his lunch."

9.3

I enter my son's room and I see orange peel, drops of soup, and breadcrumbs on the tray. Cuzco isn't there. My son is sleeping, his head tilted toward the darker side of the bed. A large diamond of light filters through the window covering part of the floor and the bed. I lean toward Teo, I caress his frosted hair, and I marvel at how little it takes to make me happy.

He turns his head toward me and then folds in on himself, he pisses his pajamas. His squinty eyes look wildly around the room.

"Grand-ma, help, help!"

"It's me, Teo, it's me."

"Some-bo-dy help me!"

He holds up his hands to block my face.

"I don't want to die yet!"

"I'm not going to do anything to you. I'm your dad."

I move my face away from his hands but they follow, not touching me, just hiding me from his view. He seems to be out of breath.

"Grand-ma!"

I grab his arms tightly. He cries out in pain.

"GRANDMA!"

I let go of him and I jump back from the bed. I knock the tray to the floor: the orange peel and seeds scatter. Cuzco enters the room without looking at me. He takes Teo's hand and gives him a kiss on the forehead. I leave the room. I sit in the hallway and rest my head on my knees until Teo stops crying.

When Cuzco reappears, I sit up straight and dry my eyes.

"He's sleeping now, sir."

"Thank you for saving me."

"It was nothing, ma'am."

"What can I do to repay you?"

Cuzco's docile hands hang at his side, he's silent.

"Tell me, Cuzco, what you would like me to do."

"I don't like to be followed. I don't like to be disrespected."

My shame is so great I can't even formulate a coherent apology. Cuzco ignores my blubbering and continues speaking.

"I could take you, if you want. Next Friday."

I tell him that I'd love to go and that I'm grateful for his trust in me. I stand up and silently help him clean up the mess left by the fallen tray. The crumbs stick to the soles of my shoes. On the way to the kitchen, I walk by the open door of the boys' room; they're playing war on the computer again, this time in a jungle landscape. Don't they ever get tired?

9.4

Moses can't stand that I'm friends with a clumsy panchama with breath like a dead rat. He found out through a friend of a colleague. "And how shameful of September, hiring him secretly." I'll never have to pass on his kind regards again. He threatens to take away the body he gave me; I know he can't do that; I just have to wait for him to get over it. I defend Cuzco but not too fervently; I don't want to lose my job and that's something Moses can take away from me. I keep my head down and copy the most relevant points from a Wikipedia article on the Dubno Raion of Ukraine; then on the swastika in Hinduism; then on New Zealand's diplomatic missions after the flood.

9.5

Men's clothes aren't as comfortable as women's but I decide I can tolerate tank tops; I still wear women's perfume though. My hair, shaved almost to my scalp, retains moisture from my shower until the sun in the street makes it disappear.

It takes me a moment to locate the doorbell at Saffron's house; at first I think they've moved it but then I remember that I'm just in a different body. That must be the first order that the brain gives out: this is your new home, there were no others before, there will be no others after. Saffron opens the door.

"Are you selling jewelry? I want a gold bracelet."

I show her the white palms of my hands and I explain that it's me, her grandmother's friend. Saffron opens her mouth and then says "No!" She jumps down the steps to give me a hug and then hangs on my shoulders for a moment.

"That's why you haven't come back to visit," she says as she releases me. We go inside and she offers me ginger lemonade. "I made it myself." All the windows and doors of the house are open; the curtains and her skirt flutter.

Of course, Saffron makes me recount all the details of the accident. She recoils at the putrid and moans at the sordid. In my tale Gorila becomes a greasy land where the panchamas want to rape old women with their dead cocks on a mattress of stolen livers and tombstones. She lies face up on the couch as she listens and tilts her head back. Her nipples won't stop eyeing me from below her cleavage.

I explain that before the burning process could be carried out they had to surgically separate my psychic structure from the dead brain it was contained in; otherwise the pain would have been intolerable. "Then they threw me into flotation so I could keep breathing, like a fish in a bucket."

"Do you remember anything?"

"I was on a very powerful sedative. It was like an uncomfortable dream."

"Like when you piss yourself in your sleep."

"Exactly. Then after that they finally burned me into this body."

"Do you know how the previous guest died?"

"No I don't. I know that the body I had before was from a woman who broke her neck in a train accident."

I regret having confessed that detail. Despite never having known her, I feel an unbreakable connection to that woman, too private to allow another person to touch her with their opinions. A good woman, who, when she died, offered the comfortable nest of her body so that I could come back to life. I wonder if she was burned in a new body or if she's still in flotation.

I take a sip of lemonade. A mint leaf sticks to my lips. Saffron leans over and removes it for me. I grab her by the waist and kiss her. She opens her mouth but then closes it. I force my tongue between her lips. She clenches her teeth.

"I'm not a lesbian! I don't want to kiss you."

"I'm a man. I was always a man."

"You're a lesbian and you're trying to seduce me!"

She presses her legs to her body and she accuses me with her bulging olive-colored eyes: "You probably died on purpose just to get a man's body so you could seduce me." I laugh at her. "It's true!" she shouts.

I tell her the truth and apologize for not having been honest from the start: that I'm the first husband of her grandmother from before she remarried, that I'd been looking for Adela's offspring for a long time, that I had been a man burned into the body of a woman because my family couldn't afford anything else. I ask if she believes me.

Saffron still has her guard up, her knees bent next to her

face and a pillow between her legs. She says yes but when I lean forward to kiss her, her swan's neck says no.

9.6

Friday again. Saffron's rejection affects me more than I'd like. You would think that living more than a hundred years would strengthen your character, but no. We are still the same primitive animals from the time we're born to the moment we die, and then after we die too.

The anticipation of the excursion to Gorila with Cuzco helps me deal with the frustration. And this time we don't have to wait until midnight. Repulsion over Cuzco's presence is unanimous in the neighborhood and was expressed in graffiti messages on the walls which September scrubbed off herself. I offered to help her but she refused. I glared with the broom in my hands as the neighbors watched her wash away their hate.

After dinner, Cuzco and I put the dishes away. He takes his time; ever since the news about him went public he's extra careful not to break any dishes. When we finish he gets his bag, which he already had packed in his room. This time we leave together and through the front door. September offers to come with us but Cuzco declines as politely as possible, without giving her any explanation. I know that she watches us leave as she sits in the dining room wrapped in a shawl of darkness.

As we travel by train to the shantytown, Cuzco tells

me about his life. When he was a boy he worked on his uncle's farm; every once in a while he had to castrate a bull or butcher a pig. He died of an illness that wasn't treated on time; he doesn't know which or doesn't remember. He pauses to bite his nails. He says he always felt comfortable in his body and, when he died, he refused the procedures of being moved to a new body. In the country they spit at him for being a panchama so he had to move to the city. He doesn't think there's anything wrong with being attached to his original body. "At the worst it's childish," he says "and there's nothing bad about that."

I ask him about the physical disadvantages. Cuzco shrugs his shoulders. "My body doesn't age anymore, but it does deteriorate; I'm going to get clumsier as the years go by. One day, my body is going to die in a horrible way, and this time I'll die with it. It seems fair to me."

We enter Gorila through a gate sculpted by street artists; wide and well lit. This time it doesn't stink so bad; my previous body must have had a better sense of smell. Cuzco points out the best stalls. At one of them, run by a coughing indigenous woman, I buy a Sega Genesis game cartridge; I think it might work to smooth things over with Moses. At another stall I run into an African man who looks exactly like me. He stares with a look of shock and hatred, glaring into my eyes as if he were trying to crush them with his gaze. My guide pulls me away by the arm.

We arrive at Cuzco's house. Despite the growing stench in the air I start to feel more comfortable as we lose the African man in the winding maze I'd be incapable of finding my way out of on my own. Cuzco hands me the rope ladder that leads to the floor above the crypt; with my new muscles it's easy to climb up. The wooden construction looks precarious but homey. A group of children sleep on mattresses on the floor.

"Kids, nephews, and grandkids," Cuzco tells me in a hushed voice so as not to wake them. Through the windows I can see the upper part of the shantytown, the bats crowding the raised walkways used to deliver merchandise to the stalls below. I hear the hum of the wind. It blows for a long time then stops and starts again. Cuzco empties the contents of his bag and fills it with clean clothes. He signals for me to follow him back down. Outside the house, he tells me that his wife has the dog with her at work. I ask him if he misses his family during the week. He doesn't answer.

We leave the shantytown, but we travel farther from the city in the opposite direction of my house. We take a bus; Cuzco pays with coins, something I haven't seen for a long time. We don't speak during the trip, we just look out the window as the buildings disappear.

We get off the bus in the middle of a field, half an hour later. We follow a line of electrical towers; we pass over a cattle guard and come to a stable. Inside, the horses sigh in their sleep.

"When I need money I sometimes come here to work for the whole weekend. See that group of lights out there?" Cuzco says to me, "Those are the owner's houses. He's a good person, like Miss September. We panchamas work for good people or we don't work at all. I work so many hours here that I don't have time to take a bath; if I did, I would miss the only bus that takes me back to your house to start the new week. I sleep out here with the horses."

I see the horses inside their stalls. A sturdy stallion asleep on his feet; standing guard for the troop. Cuzco rubs his rump.

"One night, the owner didn't know I was working and he came to the stable with a friend of his. They kissed and they had sex. I stayed quiet in my bed, holding my breath like a real dead man. Later I realized that his friend was Mr. Wales."

Cuzco bites his nails; I remain silent.

"Your grandson, Mr. Wales, he's the vet for these horses."

"Does September know?"

"I didn't want to tell Miss September."

"Does Wales know?"

"I told him I'd seen him here. He's afraid of me now. I told you before, sir: we panchamas work for good people or we prefer to beg."

Cuzco changes the horses' water and leaves a sugar cube for each one. "Now I'd like to go home, so I can spend time with my family," he tells me. The bus takes a while to arrive, but the wait gives me time to think.

9.7

I get home at dawn, tired and greasy. I take a shower in Cuzco's bathroom; the water is lukewarm and I hear the banging of the pipes. I put on the change of clothes that September set out for Cuzco; I'll leave him some of my clothes in exchange later.

I connect to the internet and I look for Vera. She's available, reading about botany in the node of a specialized digital library. Her avatar is a horse now and it reminds me of the stallion from the night at the stable. She asks me what time it is there and I ask her how many news modules have passed since she started reading; that's the way time is measured in flotation. She doesn't want to answer, she says it was too many to count. We talk about Teo's fear of my new body and I ask for her help. She agrees and I tell her that I'll let her know when everything is ready, in the meantime she can go back to her reading.

I wait in the kitchen; the news modules illustrate the problem of unemployment in young adults as a bubble about to burst. I squeeze some oranges and eat four pieces of toast with cactus jam. I've always enjoyed a shower and a good breakfast in the morning. When September appears, I ask her if she could please help me with Teo. We go into his room hand in hand so that my son won't be afraid; September's hand is as warm as a piece of toast. I carry a computer in my other hand.

Teo stares at me nervously from his bed but September soothes him. I even manage to take his hand for a second before he pulls it away. I activate the microphone and the computer speakers.

"Hello, little brother!"

The voice Vera had when she entered flotation makes me shake; maybe because it's the first time I've heard it with organic ears instead of through software.

"Ver-a! Big sis-ter!"

The computer identifies their voices and shows an image of the two of them together when they were children. I took that photo, I think; I was alive at that time. Teo sits up with his legs crossed, leaning reverently toward the screen.

"They told me you've been refusing to eat for a few days."

"Too much sun. Too much food."

"They told me you were afraid."

Teo looks at me for a second before returning his eyes to the screen.

"Yes."

"Don't be silly. It's Dad! He's just in disguise. Like when we were little and we dressed up like monsters to scare Mom."

Teo looks at me again but this time for longer before he turns back to the screen.

"Dis-guised as a pan-cake? Burnt! Burnt pancake!"

He points at me and falls backward in laughter. Tears run down the sandpaper of his face. I shout "Dirty dog pancake!" and I throw myself on top of him. Teo hugs me tight and laughs hysterically.

We leave the siblings giggling in private, like they used to when Teo was three years old and he would whisper in his sister's ear to tell her where he'd hidden his toys. September goes into the boys' room to play with them. I see Wales standing in front of the bathroom mirror, shaving. I enter the bathroom and close the door.

9.8

Wales leaves the bathroom but I remain seated on the bidet. He broke down and told me the reason that his marriage is in crisis. He wants to be burned into a woman's body. I sat down and listened to him. September doesn't know the reason, but she knows something is wrong with him. Wales is terrified that she'll find out. The pressure is too much for him to bear; he's even considered committing suicide without telling anyone so that he can get a body that's better suited to him, where he can feel truly alive.

"Your experience opened my eyes," he said. That explains why his fights with September started when I arrived. I promise I'll try to help him. Now I'm his confidant. For the first time in my life I feel like the kind of grandpa I always wanted to be.

I don't tell Wales, but I'm a coward too. Even though I have Bragueta's address, I can't get up the nerve to confront him. I even have the strength that I was lacking before. This time after leaving flotation I didn't take long at all to recover from the procedure; maybe because this body is younger, or maybe because I was only in flotation for a few days, not the better part of a century.

I can even play soccer now. The boys shout as we play in the yard. The grass scratches and stains, my thighs stretch and my knees crack, but it's different now; there's no pain or cramps or exhaustion.

10.1

Sᴇᴘᴛᴇᴍʙᴇʀ ᴇɴᴛᴇʀs ᴍʏ ʀᴏᴏᴍ in the middle of the night. I'm lying in bed, naked. I keep my eyes closed. I should be sedated but I prefer insomnia to drugs. I hear her approach me with the almost imperceptible noise of her movements. I think it would be better to stop pretending to be asleep, but it's too late. I hear September's breathing. I feel her hand caress me. She's covering me with the sheet. She shakes my shoulder.

"Rama."

I pretend to come out of a deep sleep. I open my eyes halfway: luckily my most important parts are covered by the sheet. I blink several times and pat the bed unnecessarily. September is wearing a summer nightgown, her hair is messed up and she looks sad.

"Teo is dying."

I stop pretending.

It's a sentence I've been dreading for ages. When Teo was little and I was terrified of an accident in the cradle or on the slide; when I was in flotation and I thought I'd never see him again; when I was burned into the fat lady's body and I could see that Teo was a living mummy of my son. But I didn't expect to hear that sentence today;

perhaps I expected never to have to hear it.

I walk to my son's room. I should run, but I'm not anxious to get there. I'm afraid to pass through the doorway and look in the direction of the bed. But I do pass through the door and I do look toward the bed. Wales stands to one side, motionless, feeling as useless as I felt when my dad died. Teo stares at the ceiling; he can't talk anymore. He breathes deeply.

I see it, but I don't accept it. I understand that his body will stop functioning and then his brain activity will cease. I can't fathom that everything I know as my youngest child will soon disintegrate. Internet is to blame, the state of flotation, the burned bodies; everything I represent. When I was young, people got old and died; when I was about to die, they convinced me that I couldn't; when I returned to life they gave me back my youth. Now it seems impossible to accept that someone could disappear and that this person is my son.

September cries. Wales scolds her: "It's Teo's decision," but he seems closer to death himself than his father does. His kids will be lucky because they won't have to go through this; I guess that's why they don't wake them up to say goodbye to their grandfather.

I move closer to where Teo can see me. I take his hand, but it's not the hand I held when he was the size of a guinea pig recently issued from his mother's womb. This body isn't right. Only my original body, faulty heart and all, would allow me to properly say goodbye with the right face and the right voice and the right look in my eyes. Teo lifts his hand and I rest it on my cheek. He looks at me with a serious expression; no he looks worried.

"I'm not sleep-y, Dad."

10.2

I spread the ashes from the back steps of our house. Wales is sitting where Teo always sat. September points the computer toward the scene; I hear Vera's sobs from the screen. The kids, uncomfortable, tug at the collars of their shirts. They hold a completely different understanding of what it means to have a grandfather, great-grandfather, or aunt; the old labels must seem opaque and imprecise to them. They are the last generation; from now on there won't be generations but multiplications; upward and downward, toward a new vertical structure. Upward and downward float Teo's ashes, scattered by a spring-like wind. Vera asks us to leave the computer on the steps, just a little while longer. Cuzco sweeps up the ashes that the wind returned, and he stores them in a small jar.

10.3

Wales lent me a gray shirt for the funeral. I didn't return it and as I examine my reflection in the bus window, I think it looks good on me and it's appropriate for the occasion.

I get off the bus in the neighborhood I grew up in,

where I went to high school and where I went out with my redheaded ex-girlfriend with delicate hands. The neighborhood looks like it refused to keep up with the times, getting old as the century passed. In a few years, its deterioration will be in fashion and the wealthy will want to buy the dilapidated properties and start up themed bars. Until then, it'll just be a neighborhood of loose sidewalk tiles and the smell of cat piss.

The address I wrote down is easy to find. I ring the doorbell twice. I set the briefcase on the ground as I wait and I scrape a smashed golden fruit off the sole of my shoe.

Bragueta opens the door, drying his hands on a towel. The rest of his body, even the scar of his missing eye, is stained black with grease. He asks me what I want. I lift up the briefcase.

"I'm a lawyer. My client has died and I'm here to give you the part of his inheritance that was left to you, as indicated in his will and under the current law."

"But how do you know who I am?"

"You're Zambrano."

"It's been a long time since anyone's called me by that name."

He hesitates; I shake the briefcase. He lets me into a garage where an old car has its insides exposed to the air; beyond I can see a dining room, barely separated from the garage by a broken sliding door. I sit in one of the dining chairs without waiting to be offered.

"Have you lived here long?"

Bragueta shrugs his shoulders.

"It's all in the Koseki. Did they let you see my register or not?"

"I was just trying to be polite."

I look him in the eye as I play with the clasp of the briefcase. Bragueta lowers his gaze first.

"Do you want some coffee?"

"I'd prefer a tea."

"I only have regular."

My millionaire's body must have made him feel the guilt of the poor. I make a face of disgust on purpose.

"Well, if you don't have anything else."

As the water boils Bragueta washes his hands under the faucet; I can hear him rubbing them hard. When he returns to the dining room with the tea kettle I notice that, minus his hands, the rest of him is still stained.

"Who is your client?"

"Ramiro Olivaires. Do you have sugar?"

In the reflection of a monitor I see a dirty one-eyed man and a spotless African sharing a pot of tea; it's not us. The water burns my tongue but I don't say anything.

"So Rama's dead? God, how much time's gone by? Who would've thought he'd have remembered me? Was he in flotation, or in a new body . . .?"

"We're certain that you know the status of my client," I respond as I tap the briefcase a few times. "In fact I have to verify the relationship between you two in order to be able to give you the inheritance. This is the first inheritance you've received, isn't it?"

"I didn't know anything about what happened to him," Bragueta blubbers. "Almost nothing."

"There's a new inheritance law, and if you don't cooperate . . ."

"I knew that they had burned him in a new body, but I never knew who."

"Ah."

"No one knew what body he was in, I swear, I tried to find him."

"Well why didn't you ever try to find him before, when he was in flotation?"

"I couldn't"

"Why not?"

He flattens his hair with his hand, searching for an answer he can't find.

"Understand, Zambrano, that if you want the inheritance you have to respond; if not, I'm going to have to donate it to a public institution, as stipulated by the current law."

"There was some unsettled business between us . . . it was complicated . . . from when we were alive the first time."

"What happened back then?"

Bragueta leans toward me, his one-eyed face looks more and more distorted.

"Rama was waiting on a transplant . . . it was his last chance . . . I interfered and I got the transplant first . . . even though I could have waited a little longer . . . he was my friend . . . I was scared . . . I needed it . . . he died . . ."

My white palms sweat, Wales's gray shirt sticks to me. My saliva seems thicker as I swallow. I lift up my briefcase and stand. "That's not enough," I think I say to him, and I walk toward the door.

When I reach his old car, Bragueta tries to grab the

briefcase. Unlike our meeting in Gorila, this time my mind is sharper and my body is more flexible. I smash the briefcase into his ribs and I grab him by the neck.

"You fucked me, Bragueta, son of a bitch."

The briefcase opens and my printed Wikipedia articles fall to the floor. Bragueta steps on the pages, staining them with grease as he flails his arms. I squeeze until my fingers stop slipping on his sweaty skin. I let go. He collapses against the wall and slides to the floor, he pants and coughs. I throw the empty briefcase at him. Bragueta puts up his recently-washed hands, but he doesn't look at me.

10.4

More outbreaks of courage in my family. After his father's death, Wales confesses the truth to September. I wasn't home when he did it.

The patio is already dark but the automatic light doesn't come on; and there's no glow from the computer in the study. It must be turned off for once. The night is humid. A mosquito dances on my naked torso; I don't move. September approaches with her arms crossed.

"Did you know?"

I tell her that I did. For a second I think she's going to slap me.

"You have to choose, him or me.'

"Wales is my grandson."

"That's your choice?"

I tell her no. She tells me to think about it and she goes out onto the patio without uncrossing her arms.

The mosquito bites me.

10.5

The gray shirt is stained with grease, so I put on a tank top instead. It's the same color as Saffron's eyes. When I get to her house, she's sitting on the porch, as if she were waiting, ready to berate me.

"It was my birthday and you didn't bring me a present."

From where I'm standing I can almost smell her hair.

"I'm just saving up to buy you the operation to make you look Asian."

I offer her my hand to help her up. She grabs on to my arm.

We go into her house. The family tree on the wall isn't a tree anymore but a web, and it has new inscriptions that shine differently from the others: my name is there, with my different bodies, next to her grandmother. I take her into her room: I imagined it would be black but it's all pink. Saffron sucks on me. I suck on her. She has the same taste of roots as Adela did. I put her legs on my shoulders to reach her better. I lick her feet and her ankle bracelet, the bells jingle with the thrusts like Christmas has come early. Saffron stretches and clenches her toes until she comes. I kiss her neck until she falls asleep.

10.6

I dream that Bragueta rips my heart out with his soapy hands and puts it in his mini freezer. Adela's heart is there too, but it doesn't beat like mine does. I get up, get dressed, and take the bus. The first thing I do when I get off the bus is walk by my old childhood home. The lights are off, the plants are well taken care of by someone else who lives and sleeps in the body of someone else who lived and died. I don't waste any more time. I walk from memory to Bragueta's house and I ring the bell. No one answers; he must be working in Gorila.

I rest my heavy head between my knees and I doze off. Even in summer it's still cool in the early morning while the sun takes its time coming out. Bodies are like ripe fruits, we've come a long way but we still aren't immune to temperature, or to feelings.

When Bragueta walks up and sees me he stops short; I must look like a rabid dog to him. I tell him not to be afraid and I invite him out for breakfast.

11.1

ONE OF THE BOYS BEAT the other one to death. They weren't fighting. They weren't even mad. They did it because they thought it would be fun. "To visit grandpa," said Fluorescent, covered in blood; behind him Corona's body laid waiting for the police to arrive. I tried to explain that Teo wasn't in flotation, that he hadn't even been burned into another body or anything else they could imagine. "He's probably hiding somewhere," he responded. Once I realized it was useless, I sent him to wash his hands.

The police made Wales fill out the usual forms. Before taking the body away, one of the officers scolded September: "And this better not happen again."

Two hours later the boys were chatting, one in his body and the other on the web. "It hurt a little," Corona admits, "but being in flotation is great." Fluorescent curses his luck: "I was the one who called dying first!" Wales and September silence them and they give them a long lecture about how killing isn't allowed under any circumstances. The boys say "We knooow," in unison. They agree, disappointed, that their Christmas gift will be a new body for Corona.

11.2

Saffron wants me to meet her parents. The holidays would be the ideal time. Will her dad have my wife's face? Or has he changed his body so that now there's nothing of Adela left in him? He could tell me more about her, but I don't want to know more; what I really want is to see Adela, to touch her and everything else that you can't do once someone is dead.

Saffron smokes naked in her bed. We've never been to mine; I would be embarrassed to have her over to September's house. The smoke makes me cough and her pile of dirty clothes smells like baby vomit. I'm starting to get tired of her. Maybe she's too young for me. She's growing her hair longer now and I can hardly see her neck.

11.3

Christmas is still celebrated but it now represents the cycle of birth and resurrection that is an everyday reality: we live, we die, we enter flotation, we're burned into new bodies, and then we enter flotation again. For the most conservative on the other hand, Jesus represents the liberation of the spirit from the prison of the machine. Everyone is happy in the end. I want to be happy too.

When it gets dark I go to Bragueta's. He's wearing a short-sleeved shirt and he's alone. They've already started setting off the first fireworks, even though it's still several hours until midnight.

"Happy Christmas Eve."

All the nights that I've visited him, we talked while he works on his old car. He's still scared of me and he's not sure how to answer my questions sometimes. I try to act natural. I haven't forgotten what he did to me all those years ago; but before that he was a good friend and I haven't forgotten that either. I hope to settle things over dinner.

He asks me if I brought him a Christmas present; I tell him that his present was the backpack with the wireless battery. He ignores my answer by getting up to get plates from the kitchen. Dinner is good, but I'm not hungry. The cork from the bottle of cider hits the car. We laugh. I slip a dose of the sedative they gave me when I came out of flotation into his glass.

He falls asleep with his head in the cold meat. I clean him up with a napkin and then drag him to bed, where I tie him up. While I wait, I look around the house. There's nothing old enough to mean anything to me. I find some merchandise that he must have been unable to sell: a month's supply of nutrition wafers, disposable underwater cameras, twenty-year-old subway maps, books of poetry inside an aluminum pot, scanners for labeling items on the web. Next to the car I find portable freezer, empty except for the smell of ground meat. In the kitchen refrigerator there are more low-quality regenerated organs than there is food. I put on water to boil.

I wake him up with ice cubes that I took from the freezer.

"I'm going to have your heart for Christmas dinner."

"Not again," he begs.

I think that cannibals must value human beings more than the rest of us; not only do they nourish themselves on another spirit, but they also make the most of fresh meat. I return to the kitchen, plug in a knife, and turn it up to its highest setting.

"No, please, no. I'm sorry, really."

"You stole my heart and now I'm going to take yours."

For the younger generations, leaving the flesh behind to dive into the pool of the web is a favorable prospect; these days only the weakest souls can't stand the absence of a body for very long. But for me it was a trauma that still gnaws at me.

"Do you know how much I lost because of you? My wife went off with another guy. My kids grew up without me. I was imprisoned and hungry and you never showed up. I think you should try it. You hear the water whistling? I'm going to boil you down to your bones."

Bragueta begs me, sobbing: "I promise to be a good friend, I swear."

I shove part of his shirt in his mouth so that he can't scream too loud. In the end, I can't go through with it and I just cut off one of his arms. I make him a tourniquet before I go to the bathroom. I vomit in the bathtub and then wipe my mouth with the last of his toilet paper. I drop his arm in the toilet and press the button; I watch it spin around the bowl.

I return to his room and tighten the tourniquet. "If you behave, I'll take you to the hospital." I remove the wad of shirt from his mouth. He screams but not too loud. "Come on, asshole, take me," he says. I ask him where the car keys are.

Bragueta sweats and bleeds in equal measures.

"How long has it been since you've driven a car?" he asks.

"Since you fucked me over."

I open the garage door. The car starts and stops, but I manage to control its convulsions and activate the semi-automatic drive function to the hospital.

"Don't stain the car, it's just been fixed up," I say to him. Bragueta shakes his head and murmurs incoherently.

When they ask him what happened, he repeats again and again that it happened playing soccer. The doctors don't believe him, but they're too busy with the many Christmas Eve trauma victims who've come in smelling of gun powder, eyes burst open, or hands on fire. I sit in the waiting room until they tell me that Bragueta says he's sorry but he just wants to sleep.

11.4

I hurry to make it home before my family goes to bed. Cuzco is with his family. Wales and Fluorescent play on the web with Vera and Corona. September asks me if I've eaten yet. The house is clean and smells of sweet meat. From the dining room I ask her if she wants to go outside to watch the fireworks with me.

The boys' homicide pact brought Wales and September back together. Death conquered what love couldn't. She doesn't know that he cheats on her but I'm going to follow Cuzco's lead and remain silent. September has accepted my grandson's chosen sex and Wales is going to switch to a woman's body through medical intervention. They're looking for a body that can breast-feed because Corona is going to be burned into the body of a baby so that he'll live longer which will mitigate the costs. I'm going to help them pay for it; after all, I spend very little of what I earn with Moses. Maybe we'll find a deal on the two procedures. Of all the bodies on the market, the most expensive is a young woman. As birth control advances, women are valued more and more.

12.1

So MUCH HASSLE to finally get a job and now I'm so happy when I get a few days of vacation. I run my hand under the collar of my shirt, stretch my muscles, crack my joints. I sweat. It's nice to walk through the gleaming downtown cityscape with its open-air zoo and the buildings all connected by elevated walkways; new to everyone and not just to me. As I turn off my devices, Moses says he's proud of me, in his own way: "I'm a lucky boss to have a black man like you at my service."

I go to my favorite restaurant with a pretty girl; I feel proud that it's my grandson. Men and women alike turn their heads to look at him, evaluating the cost of the body. On the social networks we pretend that Wales is my girlfriend so that Saffron will lose interest. I still care for her, but she needs to live a hundred more years of life, maybe pass through a few more bodies, as unattractive as possible. Ugliness breaks you in, I'm about to say to Wales, when I feel as if my brain lurches inside my skull. A few feet away, a man identical to me is walking into the bathroom. I sit open-mouthed as the synthetic meat I ordered slides down my esophagus. My grandson takes an emergency battery out of his pocket but I wave it away. Little by little I feel my organs return to their places. My vocal chords unknot. I excuse myself and stand up to go to the bathroom.

When I open the door I don't see anyone. I look at myself in the mirror: the whites of my eyes are dark yellow. There's a mop bucket in front of the urinals. I look into the stalls. Only one has a closed door. I knock. The person who opens the door is my reflection, but distorted like only a brother could be. The same in every way, only with a slightly different nose and the green jumpsuit he's wearing. He stares at me, immobile with a bag in his hands.

I'm on the floor before I realize what happens. The bag over my head keeps me from breathing; I try to escape but I can't. I'm not strong enough. My suit is wet with either water, piss, or floor cleaner.

12.2

I'm a horse; yellow, or maybe red, I can't see color. But my eyes can look in two directions. The horizon is wide and flat. I can see my food; all I need to see, and what I can't see, I smell, I hear, I feel. Stomps, wheels, whistles, voices, and storms.

Cuzco gives me hay, rubs my sides; he's the only one I let ride me. I take him far and I feel happy. Like when I jump, with my four hooves suspended in the air. Left foot, left hand, right foot, right hand, suspension.

Moses denies any guilt on his part: "If I'd known that the body had come from the black market I would have reported it."

Instead of burning me into another body, Moses wanted me to be part of an experiment. He thinks it might offer a solution to all the reincarnated who suffer the sensation of phantom parts that their bodies never had, he says. "Maybe there are people who would be happier as octopi; maybe each of us has, inscribed in our genes, the true animal that we should be, and human is just one option of many." Moses wants me to be his Trojan horse. I like it. Existence is too long to keep the same job forever. Left foot, left hand; right foot, right hand.

A mare in heat: we snort at each other. I like the smell of excrement and urine. I masturbate, rubbing my penis against my stomach. I hate the smell of bones, it stops me dead in my tracks: wherever there's the stench of death, there are predators. Left foot, left hand; right foot, right hand, suspension.

My grandson comes to visit; he's also my veterinarian now. He shakes his head; it must be nice to have a female wife and a male lover. September tells me that Vera wants to be a horse and she is going to take the body of one of my colts. That makes me happy too. The heat of the sun, suspension.

Vera calls me "Dad." Wales calls me "Grandpa." September calls me "Ramiro." The boys call me "Rama." Cuzco still calls me "sir." The other horses don't call me anything. I can sense my ego melting away. The last phantom member dissolves.

Martín Felipe Castagnet was born in La Plata, Argentina, in May 1986. He holds a PhD in Literature from the National University of La Plata and is currently Associate Editor of *The Buenos Aires Review*. *Bodies of Summer*, his first novel, won the Saint-Nazaire MEET Young Latin-American Literature Award and has also been translated into French and Hebrew.

Frances Riddle is an editor and translator based in Buenos Aires, Argentina.

MICHAL AJVAZ, *The Golden Age.*
The Other City.

PIERRE ALBERT-BIROT, *Grabinoulor.*

YUZ ALESHKOVSKY, *Kangaroo.*

FELIPE ALFAU, *Chromos.*
Locos.

JOE AMATO, *Samuel Taylor's Last Night.*

IVAN ÂNGELO, *The Celebration.*
The Tower of Glass.

ANTÓNIO LOBO ANTUNES,
Knowledge of Hell.
The Splendor of Portugal.

ALAIN ARIAS-MISSON, *Theatre of Incest.*

JOHN ASHBERY & JAMES SCHUYLER,
A Nest of Ninnies.

ROBERT ASHLEY, *Perfect Lives.*

GABRIELA AVIGUR-ROTEM,
Heatwave and Crazy Birds.

DJUNA BARNES, *Ladies Almanack.*
Ryder.

JOHN BARTH, *Letters.*
Sabbatical.

DONALD BARTHELME, *The King.*
Paradise.

SVETISLAV BASARA, *Chinese Letter.*

MIQUEL BAUÇÀ, *The Siege in the Room.*

RENÉ BELLETTO, *Dying.*

MAREK BIENCZYK, *Transparency.*

ANDREI BITOV, *Pushkin House.*

ANDREJ BLATNIK, *You Do Understand.*
Law of Desire.

LOUIS PAUL BOON, *Chapel Road.*
My Little War.

Summer in Termuren.

ROGER BOYLAN, *Killoyle.*

IGNÁCIO DE LOYOLA BRANDÃO,
Anonymous Celebrity.
Zero.

BONNIE BREMSER, *Troia: Mexican Memoirs.*

CHRISTINE BROOKE-ROSE,
Amalgamemnon.

BRIGID BROPHY, *In Transit.*
The Prancing Novelist.

GERALD L. BRUNS,
Modern Poetry and the Idea of Language.

GABRIELLE BURTON, *Heartbreak Hotel.*

MICHEL BUTOR, *Degrees.*
Mobile.

G. CABRERA INFANTE, *Infante's Inferno.*
Three Trapped Tigers.

JULIETA CAMPOS, *The Fear of Losing Eurydice.*

ANNE CARSON, *Eros the Bittersweet.*

ORLY CASTEL-BLOOM, *Dolly City.*

LOUIS-FERDINAND CÉLINE,
North.
Conversations with Professor Y.
London Bridge.

MARIE CHAIX, *The Laurels of Lake Constance.*

HUGO CHARTERIS, *The Tide Is Right.*

ERIC CHEVILLARD, *Demolishing Nisard.*
The Author and Me.

MARC CHOLODENKO, *Mordechai Schamz.*

JOSHUA COHEN, *Witz.*

FOR A FULL LIST OF PUBLICATIONS, VISIT: www.dalkeyarchive.com

EMILY HOLMES COLEMAN, *The Shutter of Snow.*

ERIC CHEVILLARD, *The Author and Me.*

ROBERT COOVER, *A Night at the Movies.*

STANLEY CRAWFORD, *Log of the S.S. The Mrs Unguentine.*
Some Instructions to My Wife.

RENÉ CREVEL, *Putting My Foot in It.*

RALPH CUSACK, *Cadenza.*

NICHOLAS DELBANCO, *Sherbrookes.*
The Count of Concord.

NIGEL DENNIS, *Cards of Identity.*

PETER DIMOCK, *A Short Rhetoric for Leaving the Family.*

ARIEL DORFMAN, *Konfidenz.*

COLEMAN DOWELL, *Island People.*
Too Much Flesh and Jabez.

ARKADII DRAGOMOSHCHENKO, *Dust.*

RIKKI DUCORNET, *Phosphor in Dreamland.*
The Complete Butcher's Tales.

RIKKI DUCORNET (cont.), *The Jade Cabinet.*
The Fountains of Neptune.

WILLIAM EASTLAKE, *The Bamboo Bed.*
Castle Keep.
Lyric of the Circle Heart.

JEAN ECHENOZ, *Chopin's Move.*

STANLEY ELKIN, *A Bad Man.*
Criers and Kibitzers, Kibitzers and Criers.
The Dick Gibson Show.
The Franchiser.

The Living End.
Mrs. Ted Bliss.

FRANÇOIS EMMANUEL, *Invitation to a Voyage.*

PAUL EMOND, *The Dance of a Sham.*

SALVADOR ESPRIU, *Ariadne in the Grotesque Labyrinth.*

LESLIE A. FIEDLER, *Love and Death in the American Novel.*

JUAN FILLOY, *Op Oloop.*

ANDY FITCH, *Pop Poetics.*

GUSTAVE FLAUBERT, *Bouvard and Pécuchet.*

KASS FLEISHER, *Talking out of School.*

JON FOSSE, *Aliss at the Fire.*
Melancholy.

FORD MADOX FORD, *The March of Literature.*

MAX FRISCH, *I'm Not Stiller.*
Man in the Holocene.

CARLOS FUENTES, *Christopher Unborn.*
Distant Relations.
Terra Nostra.
Where the Air Is Clear.

TAKEHIKO FUKUNAGA, *Flowers of Grass.*

WILLIAM GADDIS, JR., *The Recognitions.*

JANICE GALLOWAY, *Foreign Parts.*
The Trick Is to Keep Breathing.

WILLIAM H. GASS, *Life Sentences.*
The Tunnel.
The World Within the Word.
Willie Masters' Lonesome Wife.

GÉRARD GAVARRY, *Hoppla! 1 2 3.*

ETIENNE GILSON, *The Arts of the Beautiful.*
Forms and Substances in the Arts.

C. S. GISCOMBE, *Giscome Road.*
Here.

DOUGLAS GLOVER, *Bad News of the Heart.*

WITOLD GOMBROWICZ, *A Kind of Testament.*

PAULO EMÍLIO SALES GOMES, *P's Three Women.*

GEORGI GOSPODINOV, *Natural Novel.*

JUAN GOYTISOLO, *Count Julian.*
Juan the Landless.
Makbara.
Marks of Identity.

HENRY GREEN, *Blindness.*
Concluding.
Doting.
Nothing.

JACK GREEN, *Fire the Bastards!*

JIŘÍ GRUŠA, *The Questionnaire.*

MELA HARTWIG, *Am I a Redundant Human Being?*

JOHN HAWKES, *The Passion Artist.*
Whistlejacket.

ELIZABETH HEIGHWAY, ED., *Contemporary Georgian Fiction.*

AIDAN HIGGINS, *Balcony of Europe.*
Blind Man's Bluff.
Bornholm Night-Ferry.
Langrishe, Go Down.
Scenes from a Receding Past.

KEIZO HINO, *Isle of Dreams.*

KAZUSHI HOSAKA, *Plainsong.*

ALDOUS HUXLEY, *Antic Hay.*
Point Counter Point.
Those Barren Leaves.

Time Must Have a Stop.

NAOYUKI II, *The Shadow of a Blue Cat.*

DRAGO JANČAR, *The Tree with No Name.*

MIKHEIL JAVAKHISHVILI, *Kvachi.*

GERT JONKE, *The Distant Sound.*
Homage to Czerny.
The System of Vienna.

JACQUES JOUET, *Mountain R.*
Savage.
Upstaged.

MIEKO KANAI, *The Word Book.*

YORAM KANIUK, *Life on Sandpaper.*

ZURAB KARUMIDZE, *Dagny.*

JOHN KELLY, *From Out of the City.*

HUGH KENNER, *Flaubert, Joyce and Beckett: The Stoic Comedians.*
Joyce's Voices.

DANILO KIŠ, *The Attic.*
The Lute and the Scars.
Psalm 44.
A Tomb for Boris Davidovich.

ANITA KONKKA, *A Fool's Paradise.*

GEORGE KONRÁD, *The City Builder.*

TADEUSZ KONWICKI, *A Minor Apocalypse.*
The Polish Complex.

ANNA KORDZAIA-SAMADASHVILI, *Me, Margarita.*

MENIS KOUMANDAREAS, *Koula.*

ELAINE KRAF, *The Princess of 72nd Street.*

JIM KRUSOE, *Iceland.*

AYSE KULIN, *Farewell: A Mansion in Occupied Istanbul.*

EMILIO LASCANO TEGUI, *On Elegance While Sleeping.*

LUCIAN DAN TEODOROVICI,
Our Circus Presents . . .

NIKANOR TERATOLOGEN, *Assisted Living.*

STEFAN THEMERSON, *Hobson's Island.*
The Mystery of the Sardine.
Tom Harris.

TAEKO TOMIOKA, *Building Waves.*

JOHN TOOMEY, *Sleepwalker.*

DUMITRU TSEPENEAG, *Hotel Europa.*
The Necessary Marriage.
Pigeon Post.
Vain Art of the Fugue.

ESTHER TUSQUETS, *Stranded.*

DUBRAVKA UGRESIC, *Lend Me Your Character.*
Thank You for Not Reading.

TOR ULVEN, *Replacement.*

MATI UNT, *Brecht at Night.*
Diary of a Blood Donor.
Things in the Night.

ÁLVARO URIBE & OLIVIA SEARS, EDS.,
Best of Contemporary Mexican Fiction.

ELOY URROZ, *Friction.*
The Obstacles.

LUISA VALENZUELA, *Dark Desires and the Others.*
He Who Searches.

PAUL VERHAEGHEN, *Omega Minor.*

BORIS VIAN, *Heartsnatcher.*

LLORENÇ VILLALONGA, *The Dolls' Room.*

TOOMAS VINT, *An Unending Landscape.*

ORNELA VORPSI, *The Country Where No One Ever Dies.*

AUSTRYN WAINHOUSE,
Hedyphagetica.

CURTIS WHITE, *America's Magic Mountain.*
The Idea of Home.
Memories of My Father Watching TV.
Requiem.

DIANE WILLIAMS,
Excitability: Selected Stories.
Romancer Erector.

DOUGLAS WOOLF, *Wall to Wall.*
Ya! & John-Juan.

JAY WRIGHT, *Polynomials and Pollen.*
The Presentable Art of Reading Absence.

PHILIP WYLIE, *Generation of Vipers.*

MARGUERITE YOUNG, *Angel in the Forest.*
Miss MacIntosh, My Darling.

REYOUNG, *Unbabbling.*

VLADO ŽABOT, *The Succubus.*

ZORAN ŽIVKOVIĆ , *Hidden Camera.*

LOUIS ZUKOFSKY, *Collected Fiction.*

VITOMIL ZUPAN, *Minuet for Guitar.*

SCOTT ZWIREN, *God Head.*

AND MORE . . .